AFTER
IMPACT

AFTER IMPACT

Nicole Stark

ISBN: 1512370479
ISBN-13: 978-1512370478

Library of Congress Control Number: 2015912176

First Edition

10 9 8 7 6 5 4 3 2 1

DEDICATION

For God, my savior, and Mom, who has supported me in all my endeavors and never stopped believing in me.

Chapter One

Year 2170

A loud siren woke Avalon up.

What's wrong?

Avalon shivered and convulsed as a mysterious liquid flowed past her arms and legs. Cold air assaulted her nostrils. She was lying down on an icy metallic surface, her arms positioned on either side of her body.

Am I dead? Is this some sort of out of body experience?

Avalon struggled to open her mouth and scream but something was stuck in her throat, preventing her. As she attempted to rise up, she was met with impregnable resistance in the form of metal restraints.

No. I am definitely alive. Although I don't know for how much longer.

Someone spoke in the darkness.

"I am here," the soothing voice said. "Don't worry. You're going to be OK."

Who the heck are you? Oh my gosh is this a serial killer?

Avalon's thoughts fell to her father and her stomach tightened.

Why is my mouth closed? How come I can't see? Where is Dad? Something is wrong.

Avalon continued to thrash against the restraints.

"Don't worry, you aren't blind. It happens to everyone when they wake from cryosleep," the voice said. "You will be able to see better in an hour as the ointment wears off your eyes."

Cryosleep. Cryosleep. Doesn't that mean I was frozen? Her mind struggled to remember the past. She remembered her Dad. His eyes were sad as he handed her something. Before she could discern what it was, the image shifted to a long drive to a place she had never been before.

Someone uncuffed her wrists and ankles and removed various IV lines. Avalon curled and uncurled her fingers, stretching them out. Finally, the thing that was in her throat was removed and she gagged. Her throat was so sore, so scratchy.

Now is the time to flee. But I still can't see.

After opening her eyes over and over again, the obscured view began to focus. When the person attached to the voice blocked her line of sight, she followed the movements with her head.

But on second thought, I don't know where I am or why I am here. Where would I go? I need to play it calm.

Avalon's once frigid body temperature quickly warmed up, and with it, more of her senses returned.

What is that smell!

Alcohol, sanitizer, air freshener, and the pungent odor of human sickness slapped her in the face causing her nose to curl upwards as her lips curled down.

The voice laughed.

Glad someone thinks this is funny. They won't for long, though. Not once I clearly see their face.

After a few more moments passed, Avalon attempted to sit up. Her arms felt a little rubbery, like they could barely support the weight, but she maintained the posture until her arms felt solid again.

Something cold and metallic latched onto Avalon's left wrist, causing her to twitch for a minute with alarm.

What is that?

The voice seemed to read her mind as it answered, "Don't worry. This is just a smartwatch monitor for your vitals. I suggest you calm down as your pulse rate is very high."

The voice wrapped a warm blanket around her and assisted her in rising from her cryochamber to sitting down in a chair. Clutching her throat, Avalon gestured for water and listened to the sound of padded footsteps leaving the room. A minute later, she sipped water from a cup.

After taking a few slow sips, Avalon downed the rest in one gulp and said with a hoarse voice, "Thank you." The voice brought her some more water before she asked for it. After finishing the second cup, Avalon asked, "Who are you and where am I?"

"The name's Ilium," he said. His voice had a nice tenor to it, not too loud or too soft. "And I am a physician."

You look way too young to be a physician. You are twenty-two years old max.

"I know you have a lot of questions. Most people do after waking. However, I need you to remain calm," he requested.

That's easy for you to say. You weren't tied down, with a random stranger in front of you.

"Do you remember anything about the past?" Ilium asked.

Avalon racked her brain for memories. She had a hard time remembering her own name, much less the mumbo jumbo Ilium wanted. However, it wasn't long before distorted images began taking proper shape as they resurfaced bit by bit from the deep recesses of her foggy cognizance.

She remembered someone standing over her, placing some kind of mask over her face. Images of long nights staring through a telescope with her father emerged, tracking something. More images flooded her mind, like skiing down a pearly white slope in the Andes, barbecuing and fireworks on the Fourth of July, swimming in the neighbor's pond, and crisp orange leaves falling to the ground.

Yet, uncertainty chased her about how she came to be here. She remembered the sound of someone calling out a long laundry list of names, someone her brain recognized but whose name she could not recall.

That man. The one always standing on a podium or surrounded by flags. He must be important. Who is he?

Avalon shuddered as her pulse raced again. Her father would never let her enter a place like this alone. Shaking her head she answered, "I don't remember anything about this place. Where am I?"

"You are in Humanity's One Plan for Escape, otherwise known as HOPE habitat. The HOPE habitat is designed to protect you and about five thousand others from an extinction level asteroid."

She pivoted her head towards Ilium as fresh tears formed in her eyes.

Her father detected the asteroid one of those times he looked through her telescope. She remembered it clearly now—he later alerted the President and media outlets to the asteroid's collision course with Earth. Avalon wiped her cheek with the back of her hand and tried to ignore the ache forming inside her chest at the memory of her father.

"I know it's a lot to take in. Take your time," Ilium said.

Avalon gazed around the room. "Where is Dad?" she asked.

Ilium's face looked confused, as though she said something wrong.

"I'm sorry. I thought you remembered."

"Remember what?"

Ilium's eyes betrayed an emotion his lips didn't want to relay.

He took a deep breath before saying, "Your father was denied entry. Remember?"

Avalon continued to examine her mind for memories. But most of her memories consisted of events far precluding anything to do with this place.

"Denied? What do you mean?"

Ilium's pained expression answered for him.

"Only those between the ages of eighteen to twenty-five were allowed entry, barring the President and the head scientist Viggo."

Avalon's lower lip trembled. Tears formed in her eyes.

"You mean to tell me that my father left me in here *alone*?"

Avalon's mother died shortly after giving birth. Diagnosed with a heart problem which required powerful medicines—medicines that would have aborted the fetus growing inside of her, Avalon's mother, Margery, chose to ignore her doctor's advice and do nothing to harm her chances of bearing a child after being told of her infertility since her teenage years.

As Avalon grew up, she often wondered what life would have been like for her father if her mother had lived, and she had never been born. She usually had these feelings when she caught him staring off into a distant place or caressing her mother's photo on the fireplace mantle. Most men of his stature and rapport would have hired a nanny to help out, but her father always believed in separation of work and home. Despite his ever-increasing workloads, he prepared home cooked meals every other day. Her father made huge sacrifices throughout his life to support her, and he never remarried.

"Not alone. Like I said, five thousand others are present."

Avalon shook her head from side to side. She took the biodegradable cup and squished it in between her hands. It didn't satisfy her anger. She wanted to squish something else. Perhaps, the President's skull.

After a gut-wrenching sob, she shouted, "You think I give a rat's butt about anyone else? I only care about my father you moron!"

"I understand your reaction," Ilium said.

"Reaction? Reaction. Oh, I can *show* you reaction," Avalon said.

"Please remain seated. I would hate to have to take measures to ensure your safety."

Avalon flung her arms around and screamed. He had to be wrong. The few memories she held were threatening to devolve into a pool of pain, loss, and fear. She waited for her father to bust through the doors and come rescue her. For any signs of her friends or family. The thought that she would never see them again chilled her to the bone.

"Who are you *really* anyways?" Avalon spat. "You're too young to be a doctor." Avalon's eyes searched frantically around the room as she began yelling, "Where is the doctor?"

"Please, Ms. Adams. I am the doctor. I'm young because I skipped high school."

Avalon closed her eyes. She had to collect herself. Yelling at this crazy was not going to work. Perhaps, if she asked more nicely, he would budge.

"Where is the President? I would like to speak with him," she said with a tight-lipped smile.

"Don't worry. You will see the President today. But not in this state."

Avalon gritted her teeth in a desperate struggle to suppress her frustration. Ilium reached into a dresser and retrieved brown scrubs, socks, and black combat boots. "These are for you," he said placing them on her lap. "I am going to leave the room for a minute, so you can get dressed in private."

Avalon listened to the soft echo of footsteps as he left the room. Her eyesight was still a bit fuzzy, but she detected a few more colors and the general outline of a shirt from the clear hole in the center and at the two sides. She placed the shirt over her head first and slid her leotard off underneath it. After feeling around for the tag, which she placed on the back end of her rear, she slid her pants on. The socks were a much simpler affair. Last, she stuck her foot in each shoe to discern left from right and placed the correct shoe on the correct foot.

"I am done now," she eked out.

After returning to the room, Ilium said, "Great. You're coming around quickly."

Not quickly enough.

Avalon took a deep breath. "The alarms. Why were they going off when I woke up?"

"We think something's wrong with the wiring in the building. We are trying to fix it, and our patchwork lasts for a couple of days, but the cryochambers have been prematurely opening on occasion."

Avalon chewed on what he said for a moment before asking her next question.

"Cryochambers." Avalon looked back at the pod from which she emerged. "How long have I been in that thing?"

"One hundred years."

Avalon took a deep breath. All she had ever known, all of her friends and family, were long dead. She truly entered this habitat alone.

Avalon felt like her sanity was slipping, slipping from her fingers with every word Ilium spoke. Avalon cried silently in anguish over her whole world collapsing.

Ilium walked over to her and placed a hand on her shoulder.

Avalon knocked it off.

"Don't try to comfort me. I need to process this alone."

Ilium backed away. He didn't look angry at her brush off, but concerned.

Avalon still didn't know nor trust this "physician". Yet, if what he said were true, she was going to need more information.

After a few deep breaths, she closed her eyes. If her father truly had left her here in order to survive alone, she needed to remain calm. Between sniffles, she asked, "How many others are awake?"

"At present, around one thousand and forty-eight members awake."

Of course, that number didn't mean anything. She was pretty certain she didn't know anyone here. So she was still alone, even if there were other warm bodies physically inhabiting the space.

Ilium continued, "The President and the Council believe it's best for people to acclimate to the habitat via smaller groups, without having to deal with everyone all at once." In his calm voice, he added, "Every three months we wake up twelve hundred and fifty people. By the end of the year, all five thousand members will be awake."

Avalon swiveled her head to study the room in greater detail. Column after column and row after row of cryochambers filled the room.

Avalon wiped the tears from the corners of her eyes and returned her gaze to Ilium. "The Council? Who all comprises the Council?"

"The Council consists of six cryogenic members chosen to be awakened first. They all awoke ten years prior to us, so they are between 28-35 years old now."

"What? Why six members? And why were they awakened early?"

"Each member represents one of the six main occupations in the habitat. Agriculture, Medical, Engineering, Energy, Entertainment, and Terraforming.

They were awakened earlier in order to lay the groundwork for the rest of us to complete the mission."

Avalon's stomach growled. She moved her hand towards it, in a desperate effort to quiet the rumblings.

"You need real food now that you're awake, so I am going to leave you briefly to bring you some soup," Ilium said.

After five minutes, he returned with a bowl of chicken noodle soup. He sat it on a table next to her. The smell wafted to her nose, making her stomach growl even more. Avalon grabbed the bowl and sipped on its contents.

Canned. Yuck! But what can I expect in this rat motel.

Avalon sat in silence for the next few minutes as her vision progressed from seeing shapes and outlines to distinguishing Ilium's facial structures. Ilium's wavy black hair was in stark contrast to his ivory skin.

Avalon took another sip of soup when a little bit wasted on her scrubs. *It's so dark in here!* "Is it me or are the lights dim?" Avalon asked.

"No, it's not you. We rely on solar power, and we also conserve energy by keeping the lights dim."

"Can I have a napkin?" Avalon asked.

Ilium tore off a paper towel from a dispenser and Avalon dotted her shirt with it.

Everything in the spacious room with cement grey floors was glossy and shiny. Her gaze turned back towards Ilium and lingered a moment longer than it should have. Heat rose up within her, and she looked away.

Her attention diverted back to a phrase he spoke earlier. *He said I woke up early.*

"When was I supposed to wake up?" Avalon asked.

"You were supposed to be a part of the crew set to wake up at the sixth-month mark," Ilium said.

The six-month mark. Why so late?

"Do you feel like standing up?" Ilium asked.

Avalon placed her bowl of soup on the table beside her and slowly rose to her feet. As she took one step after another, her left foot slipped. Ilium grabbed her by the arm and caught her before she fell.

"Easy now," Ilium said while taking in her face and those lips shaped like a cupid's bow.

"Why don't you sit here for a minute," Ilium said as he eased her back down into the chair.

"Thanks," Avalon said. *Funny what one hundred years of cryosleep could do to a girl.*

Her eyesight had vastly improved since first waking. Ilium was clearly a head taller than her and his complexion was paler than her olive tone.

Panic seized her as she realized she had no idea what she looked like after 100 hundred years of cryosleep. *Do I look like a prune?*

"May I see a mirror please?" she asked.

Ilium reached into a drawer and handed her a small mirror. Her cheekbones were still plump and sat high on her face. Her brown eyes still held that elusive dewy look of youth.

After she returned the mirror to him, her gaze floated upwards towards a large digital wall clock. The bright red numbers it displayed were clearly counting down.

Avalon pointed to the clock. "What's that?"

"The countdown clock."

Avalon's brows furrowed. "What is it counting down to?"

"Until we go outside again," Ilium answered nonchalantly, as he had likely given this information several times before.

Avalon continued to stare at the bright red display. "That is pre-set, correct? Determined by an AI algorithmic formula?"

Ilium nodded as he continued to analyze her vitals on his tablet.

"Not much longer till we go outside and walk the Earth again," Avalon said. Although she knew the Earth they would return to would be nothing like the Earth she left. The one where she listened to the crunch of leaves underfoot in fall or watched as deer grazed the land. No...it would be drastically different.

"No. Not at all. I would say you woke up in an exciting time. With nine months left on the countdown clock, there is a lot of preparation left to do. You will be of great assistance."

Avalon nodded. Her eyes examined the room around her again, at all of the cryochambers still sealed away. Her nose scrunched and her eyes narrowed.

"What happened to the others whose cryochambers opened prematurely?"

The look in Ilium's soft eyes revealed she wouldn't like the answer.

Avalon reflected on the cutting-edge technology that mankind pinned its hopes upon to overcome certain extermination more than a century ago. Those who both chose and were selected to undergo this brave and perilous endeavor were thoroughly debriefed on the extensive risks and the odds that some of them might never wake up in the next century. Nonetheless, people took gambles all of the time on things with worse probability. In order to survive near-certain annihilation, a fifty percent chance of never waking were pretty good odds.

"We all knew that there would be some unavoidable casualties. This whole cryogenic and thawing process is still somewhat experimental, unfortunately," Ilium said.

The word casualty brought all of the other casualties of the asteroid. Parents left behind. Children left behind. Friends. Pets too. Avalon was to spend the next nine months of her life in this place. Tears formed in Avalon's eyes. Suddenly, Ilium retrieved a 20 gauge needle from a recessed drawer in the metal walls.

Her eyes widened. "What in the world are you doing with *that*?" Avalon asked, her voice rising in pitch.

"Please don't be alarmed," he replied with amusement, "I forgot to administer your shot. Everyone has to have it."

"Why?" Avalon looked skeptical.

"It helps prevent diseases amongst the population and also provides a year's supply of Vitamin D," Ilium answered.

Avalon's smartwatch beeped, prompting Ilium to grab her wrist and read the data.

"Avalon, I need you to calm down. You had a perfect pulse of seventy-five. Now it is one hundred and thirty."

Avalon lowered her pulse by humming to some of her favorite songs. As her pulse settled down, Ilium grabbed a tablet.

"For verification purposes, your name is Avalon Adams, you are eighteen years old, five feet seven inches in height, and weigh 120 pounds, correct?"

"That is correct," Avalon answered, never letting her eyes leave the needle in his right hand.

Ilium placed his tablet down on a metal table and prepped Avalon's arm with an alcohol wipe. He scanned her arm with a tablet, illuminating the perfect vein. "Take a deep breath," he instructed as he thumped the vein with his index finger to plump it up. Avalon turned her head away from the gleaming piece of metal about to pierce her skin.

"If that thing hurts me, I am going to have to return the favor," she joked.

"It's over!" Ilium smiled no sooner than she finished speaking. He wore a handsome smile, one that reached his eyes and formed little creases.

Avalon let out a sigh of relief. "Where's the lollipop?" she managed to ask.

Ilium smirked. He possessed boyish charm despite living in a world without parents, without siblings, and without pets. Avalon wondered what the others looked like. If their faces showed the weariness and isolation of life in the habitat. How much faster they aged physically and emotionally outside of the safety of the sleep the cryochambers offered.

"I can walk now," Avalon said, anxious to be away from the room with the needles and nauseous smells. "So, if you don't mind, can you show me to my room so I can take a shower?"

Ilium waved a small wand over Avalon which displayed a 3-D overlay image of her entire body— the heart beating, neurons firing, lungs inhaling and exhaling, and stomach digesting. Satisfied when the wand emitted a low beep, Ilium answered. "Sure, I will take you there."

He continued, "Those cryosleep chemicals sometimes play with the mind. Some people take much longer to retrieve basic memories. I am quite impressed by how fast your neurons appear to be firing. Follow me," he said grabbing her hand as they exited through the glass door. "I don't want you to fall," he stated somewhat sheepishly, but his cheeks turned a red hue at their sudden propinquity.

Walking down the rather roomy metallic corridor, he stepped through a glass door as they entered into one of the dormitories. Capsule beds, like the ones more common to Japanese culture, lined the walls. The rectangular beds featured a square metallic frame with glass in the middle and a handle for entering it on the right side. Beneath each bed was a black plate with etched in numbers. Her bed plate read AX97. A few steps were built on the left side of the capsule doors. The interior dimensions of each capsule were about four feet tall, four feet wide, and seven feet long and featured its own light switch.

"Six people are usually assigned to a room, three on each side. I know the rooms are less spacious than what you were probably accustomed to at home, and allow very little by way of privacy, but you're quite lucky. For now, due to your odd number, you currently live in this dorm alone," he said. "To conserve water, the showers automatically shut off after ten minutes because it takes that long to recycle it. If you need me for anything else, just tap the button on your smartwatch."

Avalon smiled at him as the door closed behind him before undressing.

Avalon entered the bathroom and turned on the shower head. The water temperature and pressure were preset and could not be regulated. Avalon closed her eyes as the water flowed over her. The sound of the water helped her to relax. As she relaxed, memories floated back of her entering the habitat.

"I will be with you in spirit," her father said as he kissed Avalon on the cheek. Her father hugged her tightly. Hot tears streamed down Avalon's face, but she bit the inside of her cheek to

hold them back. The President double checked the list of names boarded. Russian, Chinese, African, and Latin American names were all called.

"Avalon Adams," the President called.

Avalon's stomach fell. She was supposed to move her feet and enter the habitat to become a human popsicle, but she could not move.

"Sweetheart, I've already discussed this. I am too old to go with you. You are the future and you have to go," her father stated, placing his arms around her shoulders.

"I don't have to go. I can stay here with you," Avalon said folding her arms across her chest.

"Stay behind to do what? Die?" her father asked.

"It's what you are doing!" Avalon cried.

"Please. Don't make this any harder," her father said, his eyes shimmering.

Avalon hugged him one last time before she straightened her back and walked towards the habitat.

Her father gave her a personal effect—a necklace with a large sphere metallic bauble. Each person could only bring one personal effect with them into the HOPE habitat.

"I am sure this will give you great comfort and encouragement," her father said.

She did not know how on Earth he figured a necklace would give her comfort, but she slipped it on around her neck. It was the last thing she would have left of him in the habitat, so it would have to be enough. Fighting back waves of sadness, she nodded and waved goodbye as she entered the habitat. Thankfully, the doctors sedated her and the other young adults as soon as they entered.

BEEP, BEEP, BEEP, the one-minute warning timer sounded, as Avalon ran the small ration of shampoo and conditioner through her hair. She just managed to rinse it out before the water shut off.

She stood standing in the shower thinking about the cold new environment and her father. Tears fell down her face as she sobbed gut-wrenchingly. She wasn't used to making new friends. At her old school she had known everyone in the class since kindergarten. It still didn't mean they liked her. In fact, they often disliked her because of her intelligence. She had begged her father to let her be home-schooled, but he insisted on a public school education saying it would make her a more well-rounded person in the end. Not that any of that mattered anymore.

Eventually, Avalon stepped out of the shower, and she wrapped a towel around her body and a second one around her long damp brunette hair. Upon returning to her room, she placed on a clean pair of scrubs which were located in a drawer tucked into the wall next to her bed. Avalon looked on the wall, and then in some drawers for a blow-dryer. Nothing.

Figures. Energy conservation and all that jazz.

It could have served as another thing to make her snap, like dry grass in the forest on a hot day. But she bit her tongue until it drew blood. She didn't want to cry anymore today. She was going to have to get used to this place, and that meant trying to keep her emotions in check.

She slipped under the covers of her bed and rested for a minute. Of course, all she could think about was how she was stuck, one hundred years in the future, buried in a mountain, with no friends or family. To comfort herself, she began to hum an old Coldplay song she and her father used to sing on long car trips.

That was another thing that didn't sit well with her peers. She rarely listened to Pop music on the satellite radio. She instead always tuned into the classics. *Kinda hard to make friends when you don't know what the latest songs are, and instead of vegging out on TV you constantly have a book in your hand. A real honest to goodness ancient book, not the ereaders we received in pre-K.*

As she hummed the second chorus, her necklace unlocked around the center, and a blue light shone.

What the heck?

About two feet from her face, a holographic message from her father played.

Hello, my sweet Avalon. I embedded this message into this necklace for you as a form of insurance. This message will auto-erase after being played once, so please listen closely.

Her father took a deep breath before continuing. *As I labored over the habitat's extensive designs and complex computer systems, I noticed some changes were being made behind my back. My access to certain areas of the blueprints was slowly taken away. I don't know what is happening in the habitat now, but my priority has always been and always will be your safety.*

Her father closed his eyes briefly before reopening

them. His tone turned more serious. *I think something suspicious is going on. Rumors abound about what this habitat is really meant for, and if they are right, you must be careful who you trust. Your life may depend on it.*

Chapter Two

Avalon bolted up in bed as her heartbeat raced. *What is going on? What changes is he referring to? Why was Dad so worried?*

Avalon jumped down from her bedchamber and stood up in her room.

This is all too much. I am stuck here, buried underground without any family or friends. I didn't fully trust this place before the message, but now I definitely can't trust anyone. Avalon's head turned swiftly at the sound of a knock on the door. She allowed entry, and Ilium walked in.

"I hope I am not disturbing you," Ilium said. "But I thought you might want to take that quick tour of the place after your shower?"

Avalon nodded. *What is his angle? He is always so nice.*

Avalon followed Ilium through her dorm door and into the main corridor.

"So this is the cafeteria. It's empty right now, by it being 1000 hours. Breakfast is served from 0800 to 0900, Lunch from 1200 to 1300, and Dinner from 1700 to 1800 sharp. No exceptions."

Avalon took in a normal cafeteria setting with rows and rows of blue tables and benches. The walls were painted a standard cream color. The floors were made of white linoleum tiles. Large fluorescent lights lined the ceiling. A large analog clock which told military time hung in the center of the room while a countdown clock hung on the opposite side of the room.

Continuing their tour, Ilium led Avalon into a large room consisting of black walls, a black floor, and a black ceiling with plenty of people wearing Virtual Reality glasses. "This is our Recreation room with more than two million game programs to choose from. You can play against the computer or against another player."

The next room on the tour was a gymnasium with a treadmill, elliptical, bikes, rowers, and a machine for pumping iron. "We are highly encouraged to exercise at least three times a day," he said. Avalon glanced at a few girls utilizing the equipment already. They wore the same cropped black yoga pants and a loose-fitting grey t-shirt. The shoes were still black combat boots, however. *Guess the budget didn't have room for too many extras in the clothing department.*

The tour continued with a walk through another set of glass doors which revealed a capacious spherical shaped room with a row of built-in computer monitors lining the walls. Everyone used their hands to interface or spoke commands and code to the computer. "This is where the workstations are. It's where we work to help keep the habitat—and us—alive. You will begin working with this group of computer scientists, programmers, and developers tomorrow morning at 0900 sharp," Ilium said.

Avalon glanced at her teammates. A girl with porcelain skin and blue hair caught her eyes first. Large black rimmed glasses framed her petite face.

"Who is this new girl you brought here?" A large, tall guy said whose shirt strained to contain his muscles.

"Hi, I'm Avalon."

The tall guy with ginger hair laughed before saying, "The name's Brody. " He offered his hand to shake. He looked her up and down before saying, "So you're the reason the sirens went off." He sported a genteel southern accent with a five o clock shadow.

Avalon managed a chuckle. Then Brody tilted his head a bit. Pointing a finger at her he said, "You're Dr. Adams kid!"

Avalon nodded her head.

"You're practically famous. If it weren't for your dad's predictions, we wouldn't even be here," he said.

Ahh. My Dad's predictions.

"It's true," Ilium said. "At the time, the idea of putting 5000 people into suspended animation for more than twenty years was preposterous. The longest anyone had been placed into such a state and survived was twenty years, but when he came to his brain had turned to mush. He did not remember his name, his family, where he lived, or even how to tie his shoelaces. Yet, somehow, your father helped figure out a way to make this all work."

Avalon did not want all of this star attention. Yes, her Dad helped plan the habitat, but he wasn't here now. And he wouldn't be again. So she wished everyone would stop talking about it.

A shorter guy with handsome almond-shaped eyes and thick spiky black hair threw a hand up as acknowledgment to her and continued to work.

Brody rolled his eyes and said, "That's Xin Tu, but we call him Xin. He's the systems administrator."

Avalon relished listening to the poetic melody of Brody's voice. After quickly glancing around the room, she asked, "Where will I be working?"

Brody pointed to a blue circle on the floor between his workstation and the station of the girl with blue hair.

"Don't worry. We'll get you up to speed," he said with a smile.

The girl with blue hair still hadn't spoken to her, despite her stealing occasional glances at Avalon. Mustering up some courage, Avalon traipsed over to her and said, "Hi, I'm Avalon."

"The name's Skylar," the girl with blue hair said in a terse tone.

"Ok. You guys keep working. I am going to continue with the tour," Ilium said as he ushered her out of the room and down the corridor again.

Ilium led Avalon to a large greenhouse room filled with plants and bright artificial LED lights. "This is where we grow our food and receive some of our oxygen. We use electrolysis to split water into hydrogen and oxygen. We breathe the oxygen that is produced as well as given off by the plants during photosynthesis, and we utilize the hydrogen as a fuel source. There is lettuce, potatoes, and wheat and most of what we grow is grown aeroponically. So yeah, we are all vegetarians now. Of course, none of this is new to you since your father designed most of all of this," Ilium said.

"Who is that guy in there with the purple scrubs?" Avalon asked, gazing at a boy with curly blonde locks. His back was turned, so she did not see his face.

"Oh, that has to be the President's son, Kael," Ilium said, but the light-hearted notes in his voice from earlier vanished. "He is an Accipio." The disdain with which he said the word Accipio was not lost on Avalon.

"What is he doing in there?" Avalon asked.

"He's probably conducting his weekly walk-through inspections."

Ilium's expression changed. "Speaking of, I must alert the President that you're here," Ilium added. Pressing a button on his smartwatch, the holographic wallscreen to the left lit up instantaneously and the President's face appeared.

"Hello, Ilium. To what do I owe the pleasure?" the President asked.

"Sir, we have a new member awake. Meet Avalon Adams," Ilium stated while nudging Avalon towards the center of the screen.

"Welcome, Avalon! I am so glad to see we have another member awake in the habitat," the President stated.

The President, who was the President of the United States of America, was forty-five years old. Viggo, the geneticist, was thirty-five years old and they were the two oldest members of the habitat, excluding the Council members.

"Thank you, sir, it's good to be awake," Avalon answered with a plastered smile she hoped he didn't see through.

"You may not remember me, but I remember you. You are the spitting image of your father, the very man who helped save humanity so many years ago. " he said.

"Thank you. Yes, I miss my father very much," she said. She struggled to hide her resentment over the fact her father was unable to enter the habitat as the resident scientist because in the months prior to entering the habitat a "spot" appeared on one of his X-rays of his lungs. Prior to that detection, they were willing to make a special exception to the age requirement. Suspended animation, with the costs and resources attached to it, was deemed not expendable for someone not expected to live much longer. So, her father recommended Viggo in his stead.

The President continued on, "Yes, and I want you to know that we all owe your father a debt. A debt that could never be repaid. Because of this, you are very special in my eyes."

Her father always called her special growing up, due in large part to her above average intelligence. As she began to reminiscence about life on the outside with her father, Avalon fought back tears by biting the inside of her cheek.

"Thank you, Mr. President," Avalon said with a plastered smile.

"Carry on then!" The President said, ending the conversation as the wallscreen returned to a simulated scene of marine life.

Ilium looked at Avalon.

"You okay?"

"Yeah," she said.

"You know you don't have to be so brave. It's scary for all of us. None of us have experience with waking up one hundred years in the future, struggling to repopulate and terraform what used to be Earth."

"But you seem so cheerful. Or at least, adjusted."

"Yeah. But remember, as a physician I have access to meds you don't," he said with a wink.

"Really?" Avalon raised an eyebrow.

"Yes, but I don't really abuse them or anything. I just wanted to see you smile."

She averted her eyes from his tender gaze. Ilium took note and glanced at his watch. "It's time to eat lunch if you're hungry?"

Avalon nodded, and the two strolled towards the cafeteria.

In the cafeteria, Avalon noticed that those who wore purple scrubs stood first in line, followed by those in brown scrubs, and last were those in grey scrubs.

Avalon looked confused. "Our scrub colors coordinate with our roles. Since you're a computer engineer, you wear brown which indicates that you're a member of the Fulcio. The Accipio class, which only consists of elected officials, wears purple. The janitors wear grey and are called Compatios," Ilium explained.

Avalon furrowed her brow.

Despite the fact that the Accipios were outnumbered by the Fulcios and Compatios, they received priority.

"You've got to be kidding me!" Avalon hissed to Ilium.

"I know, it isn't the fairest thing, but at least we aren't the Compatios," he replied. "The Fulcios and Compatios receive less food and fewer credits than the Accipios for the jobs they perform. Fewer credits means the Compatios and Fulcios receive mush while the Accipios consume synthetic meat."

Avalon bit her tongue in order not to say anything. As the new kid, it was best to lay low. Still, this place was more like a prison than a habitat.

"The trick is remembering that we are better off than the billions of people who perished outside," Ilium said.

The billions who perished. Like her Dad. Her Dad who should have been inside with her. Instead, Viggo was allowed to go.

"So, what were you like before becoming a popsicle anyways?" Ilium asked.

"I liked to swim, bake, and travel," she answered while grabbing a tray. "What about you?"

"I like to draw and paint. I was learning a little bit of krav maga too before entering here," Ilium said grabbing a tray and some silverware from behind her.

"That's impressive," Avalon said.

"You're just being nice," Ilium said, looking at her with piercing sky blue eyes. Avalon's pulse quickened as her cheeks felt hot.

Avalon and Ilium placed their trays on the stainless steel counter. Avalon advanced through the line first. After swiping her wrist across a scanner, a female voice announced, "Avalon Adams." The computer calculated her exact calorie expenditure and prepared a plate with a green salad, a baked potato, and a fruit smoothie. Avalon placed the items on her tray and waited for Ilium. Ilium received two boiled eggs, a potato, and a smoothie from the machine.

"Don't worry. All of our food is perfectly portioned out. You won't feel satiated, but you won't starve either. You just feel like you wouldn't mind having a snack," Ilium said.

"Thanks for telling me," Avalon said.

Scanning the crowd before selecting a spot to sit, Avalon noted all of the Accipios sat together and all of the Fulcios and Compatios sat together. As she passed by the others, people murmured and whispered. Some followed her movements with their eyes.

But then she noticed people weren't only murmuring about her, that some of the Accipios were also sneering at Ilium.

Snobs.

One of her trio of computer teammates waved for Ilium and Avalon to sit by them. Avalon and Ilium accepted the proffered seats on the long bench seats, their trays making a small clink noise as they sat them down on the table.

Avalon leaned towards Ilium. "I know they are staring at me because I'm the new kid. But they were also sneering at you. Is everything ok?"

Ilium grimaced before answering, "Yeah. Nothing you need to know about."

Nothing I need to know about. I need to know everything about this place and the people in it. Still, Avalon chose not to press the issue.

After Avalon greeted the rest of the gang, Skylar began chatting.

"I just can't get over what happened to Dexter," Skylar said to Ilium while taking a sip of her iced water.

"I agree." Ilium stated while taking a bite of his boiled egg.

"Who is Dexter?" Avalon asked.

Suddenly the group fell silent. Avalon felt like she had opened her mouth and asked the wrong question. Her eyes darted back and forth between Skylar and Ilium, unsure of what to do or say next.

Yay! Way to make friends!

Ilium threw a glance at Skylar before opening his mouth. "He held your role in the computer lab group before you."

"Cool," Avalon said. She desperately wanted to know what happened to this Dexter, but she also didn't want to be singled out so early.

"He passed away right before you woke up. Fortunately, you arrived just in time to take his place," Ilium answered as though he could read her mind.

Avalon took a bite of her green salad. Suddenly, her curiosity trumped all other needs. "Do you know what he passed away from?"

"They say some sort of virus. But there are rumors," Skylar said. Brody gently kicked her underneath the table.

"Rumors like what?" Avalon pressed.

Skylar's face scrunched up. Brody stared at her.

"You know what I miss?" Brody said, changing the subject.

"Wait Brody. I want to hear what Skylar was about to say," Avalon insisted.

Skylar took a long sip of water, relishing in the attention. She leaned over and said, "Well. Rumors say he was killed. That something *happened to* him."

Killed. That is a strong accusation. Unconsciously, Avalon touched her necklace.

"Who would do such a thing?" Avalon asked, her eyes wide as saucers.

"That's why I tried to change the subject," Brody said with a roll of his eyes. "There is no need in scaring the new girl time she wakes up."

"They *are* only rumors," Skylar insisted. "She deserves to know, regardless."

Avalon couldn't discern if Skylar meant to inform her or scare her. It appeared she would say anything for attention, so Avalon determined it must be a mixture of both.

"I miss the warmth of the sun on my face. Not the VR stuff, but the real sun. Haptic technology has come far, but it's still far from perfect. What about you Avalon? What do you miss?" Brody asked, trying to change the subject.

Avalon wanted to know who or what killed Dexter. Even if it was just a rumor. But she also didn't want to rock the boat. So Avalon refocused her attention on Brody and chose to think of all the things she missed. Her family. Her friends. Church. School. But stating any of the above would lead to an uncontrollable crying session, so she chose to talk about food.

"I miss homemade Mac and Cheese." Several groans issued amongst the group.

"Man, that's a good one. Why'd you have to bring up food? Nana was the best cook," Brody said. "Best cakes too. She would carry those cakes to everything." Brody's eyes glazed over. "Cake cured almost all ails."

Avalon nodded her head in agreement noting the slight mist in Brody's eyes at mentioning his Grandma.

They had all lost something by coming here. No one survived without some kind of emotional scar. Though her own scars were deep, it helped to know she wasn't entirely alone. Some of the other members had memories too of their loved ones. But evidently, they just managed to focus on the mission at hand.

Avalon reflected briefly on her sweet Nana who also used to bake her cupcakes on the weekends. She didn't see her that often because she lived so far away in the Deep South. Avalon mainly visited her during the summers. The humid, sticky summers that were rescued by the delicious cold sweet tea. Her lips slightly turned upwards as she reminisced. Avalon was grateful her grandmother passed on long before the asteroid threatened the Earth.

"How do you eat that potato without any sour cream or cheese?" Avalon asked Ilium.

Ilium laughed. "You will learn how to do without a lot of things we had on the outside in due time," Ilium said.

Avalon took a bite of her potato. After chewing for a long time, she swallowed. It did not taste too bad. Still, it was no Big Greasy burger. How she missed those big, juicy burgers so filled with grease that it soaked through the paper bag. She was positive it clogged her arteries and would lead to an early death, but each time she bit into one, all her worries melted away.

Avalon's eyes wandered to the Accipio table and she noticed how much healthier they looked than the other classes. Avalon asked, "What exactly do the Accipios do here?"

"Their tasks are mostly managerial in nature," Brody informed Avalon. "There is no monetary system for remuneration here. We all receive rations for the basic necessities and barter for anything extra."

Managerial. Seemingly the AI could handle that task. Avalon finished her potato.

The holographic wallscreen lit up in front of Avalon and the whole cafeteria. Everyone became quiet as the Presidential seal appeared on the screen, followed by a close-up of the President sitting in front of his large wooden desk.

"Good afternoon," the President said.

"Good afternoon," everyone replied in unison.

"I apologize for the interruption, but I have some unfortunate news." The President folded his hands and leaned in towards the camera a little more. "Effective immediately, new work hours will be instituted. The Accipios will continue to work six hours a day, and the Fulcios will continue to work eight hours a day. However, the Compatios will need to work ten hours a day. Thank you in advance for your cooperation. Remember, the work we do is not only for ourselves, but for the very survival of humanity itself," the President's steady and monotonous voice announced.

Silence filled the cafeteria like helium fills a balloon. The President signed off, leaving the different groups to mumble about what would cause a change in workload when one Compatio stood up and shouted in protest.

"I have had enough of working all the time! Working my hands to the bone while no other group pulls their weight!"

"Shut up, you stupid Compatio!" a blonde Russian girl whose name tag read Elena Romanov yelled.

"Yeah, nobody cares. Crawl back to whatever rock you came from," said a tall African girl who sat next to Elena.

"I won't shut up! That is the problem. We don't make noise. We just sit here and take whatever is doled out to us. Well, I've had enough!" she said, slamming a hand on a table. "My friends are mysteriously abducted in the night, and yet nobody mentions anything about it. We all just act like nothing is happening!"

Elena and the trio of girls who sat at her table laughed at the words coming from the Compatio girl as they whispered the word "crazy" amongst each other.

A muscular guard, previously posted against a wall with his hands behind his back, made his way towards the slender Compatio girl and struck her back with a baton that sent strong electrical pulses coursing throughout her body. The girl's body fell down, rigid, as tears flowed from her eyes. Her emaciated body bore several bruises and scabs against copper toned skin.

Stay out of this Avalon. This is not your fight, Avalon thought. The guard with the huge biceps struck the crumpled body again, and this time no sound escaped the girl.

Still not satisfied, he raised his arm with the baton above her again.

Darn it! I can't just sit here. Avalon ran and stepped between the guard and the girl's body.

"Step away from the girl," the guard said with a low growl.

"Please, please! I believe she has learned her lesson for the day," Avalon pleaded with her arm up as though she could shield the girl on the floor.

A quiet descended over the entire cafeteria as the guard scowled at Avalon and then at the Compatio girl's crumpled body she protected.

"You are interfering with the administration of justice. That carries a penalty of a strike. Let me remind you that after three strikes you are expelled from the habitat."

"I'm sorry. I don't mean to interfere, but we can't use this Compatio girl anymore if she is dead. She's no longer speaking, so you succeeded in shutting her up." Avalon put her doe eyes to full effect on the guard. However, he did not budge.

Ilium ran and stood beside Avalon. "She's new here. I will let her know how things work."

The guard stared first into Ilium's face and then into Avalon's. Avalon's blood ran cold as she did not want Ilium in harm's way for her sake. *Why is he so nice to me? We just met, and yet here he is throwing himself on the line.*

"Humph. You better, and this better be the last outburst I hear from any of you, or else you will ALL be lined up and punished," the guard said as he lowered his baton and walked away.

Breathing a sigh of relief, Avalon slowly stepped away from the girl on the floor. Avalon looked straight ahead towards her cafeteria table and tried to ignore the stares she received. *This is exactly what I didn't want. To stand out.* After a few moments, subdued muttering began.

"Who does that new girl think she is?" said a coffee colored guard with a buzz cut who stood against the cafeteria wall with the muscular guard.

"I scanned her face. She's Avalon Adams," the muscular guard answered.

The other guard's eyes widened. "You mean Dr. Adams kid?"

"In the flesh," the muscular guard replied.

"That explains a lot. She probably thinks she runs the place just cause of her last name," the coffee-hued guard remarked.

Avalon turned to face Ilium. "You didn't have to help me," she whispered.

"I know," he answered.

Avalon was unsure of what to make of Ilium. *Why would a perfect stranger risk himself for her?*

"Thank you," Avalon said as they returned to their seats by the others. She detested being the center of attention, but she could not continue to stand idly by and allow that guard to injure that girl anymore.

"Why would you help that girl?" Skylar said as Avalon sat down.

"I just couldn't sit here and allow him to continue to injure her. But I believe we were talking about the stuff we missed before being frozen?" Avalon said, redirecting the conversation.

Judging by the look on Skylar's face, she wasn't used to someone else directing the conversation. Prior to Avalon, all the rest of the group probably followed her lead as to the topic of conversation. The air was thick between them, but she tried hard to engage the others, hoping to win Skylar's approval eventually.

After a while, the chatter resumed and once everyone finished eating, they slid their trays down the end of the table into a vacuum slot which led to a dishwasher.

"That was awesome how you handled that situation. See ya tomorrow, newbie!" Brody yelled before entering the corridor.

Ilium pulled Avalon aside as they sauntered out of the cafeteria. "You really can't do what you did today."

"What do you mean?" she asked.

"Standing up for that girl like that. You could have been hurt," he said with eyes full of worry.

"I did what was right, Ilium."

Something churned inside of Ilium's stomach at the sound of his name coming from Avalon's lips. He forced his lips into a tight line so as not to betray his budding feelings. Strange, slightly uncomfortable, but overall wonderful feelings. "I understand that. But things work a little differently here. Those guards are not our parents. They are callous and not afraid to maintain order at any cost," he said.

"I get it. They aren't here to protect us. They are here to help control us," Avalon said.

Ilium nodded.

Avalon's eyes narrowed as she said, "Explain this three strikes thing to me."

"If you commit three strikes, you get expelled from the habitat."

Getting expelled from the habitat would be disastrous. The oceans were believed to have evaporated due to the asteroid impact, and the new atmosphere was practically non-existent. The temperature would be too cold outside to support human life. Some scientists called these effects impact winter.

"And what do you have to do to deserve a strike?" Avalon asked.

"When you return to your room, search in one of your drawers. It should contain a book that explains the rules."

"Thank you," Avalon said.

Ilium whispered, "You're welcome," as she walked away.

Later that night, Avalon returned to her dorm room. After brushing her teeth and washing her face, she read through the list of rules in her drawer. The list was short and to the point. Most forms of direct insubordination, theft, etc. could earn one a strike in the habitat. Avalon doubted, however, that the President would actually utilize such severe punishments. After glancing at the time, she dimmed the light in her room and climbed up to her capsule bed.

Whereas she initially enjoyed having a room all to herself, now the room felt smaller. Claustrophobic even. She couldn't pinpoint what was off, but it made her uneasy.

Something wasn't right.

Probably just home sick. Silly me.

And she closed her eyes, completely unaware someone else was watching.

Chapter Three

Avalon dreamt of her last days before entering the habitat. Her father had asked for months what she wanted to do on that important day—perhaps, the last night of her life if she never woke up again. With such high stakes, she contemplated a trip to Tokyo or China or gambling with friends in Las Vegas. Even a trip to Disneyland in California. Thoughts of nature also occurred to her, like hiking through Yellowstone National Park. In the end, she settled on something simple.

Her father feared friends would become jealous of her "saved" status, so friends weren't allowed over. Whatever she wanted to do on her last day before entering the habitat, it could only involve her father. She had all of the clothes, shoes, purses, and gadgets a girl could ever want, and she would not need such material things in the habitat, which made a trip to the mall unnecessary. So, she opted for a father and daughter day with a trip to the local pizza parlor they had frequented every Friday for years.

On that particularly frigid day, Avalon wore black knee high boots, a black cashmere scarf, a tan Burberry trench coat belted at the waist, and black leather gloves. Her nose and cheeks were red, but her ears were protected by black earmuffs. Clouds formed and twisted overhead, casting a dreary grey shadow on everything, but at least the weatherman predicted no rain. The smell of pizza wafted into the street. Her mouth watered as her father held the door open as they entered Papa Al's Pizzeria.

"Are you sure this is what you want to do?" her father asked.

"Yep," she answered, taking off her scarf and laying it down on the booth seat.

A college age male waiter with tattoos walked up to them. "Welcome to Al's Pizzeria. Will you guys have the usual?" he asked.

"Yes."

The waiter ran to the back of the store to put in their order.

"So Dad, are you sure the AI in the habitat won't go haywire like Hal 9000 on us?"

He chuckled. "You've got quite the imagination. But, I'm pretty sure."

"What if there are human androids present that are planning a mutiny, like on Battlestar Gallactica?"

"I suggest you befriend Boomer and stay away from any cylons named Six then," he said with a smile.

The waiter returned shortly and placed a meat lover's pizza before them. They were the only customers there. Only about three waiters walked around, and they were all the owner's children. Biting into a slice of pizza, she eavesdropped as some of the waitstaff spoke Italian in a corner by the cash register. Italian was one of three languages she was fluent in, the other two being English and Japanese.

"Perché stiamo ancora lavorando? Non dovremmo essere a casa con le nostre famiglie ?" (Why are we even working? We should be home with our families.)

"Ti sto dicendo, questa cosa asteroide è solo una bufala. Stiamo chiudendo presto." (I'm telling you, this asteroid thing is just a hoax. We are closing soon.)

Her father paid the bill and as they headed out of the shop and onto the busy sidewalk, he paused. He hugged Avalon tightly. As they embraced, she inhaled his woodsy scent. A tear rolled down her face as she realized again that this would be one of the last times she would smell him.

"I love you very much. You mean the world to me. I will always be with you. Always," he said.

"I love you too," she said as her bottom lip trembled.

She awoke from her dream the next morning and yawned. She felt the sheets checking to see if they were soaked with sweat. Her heart ached from the memory of her father. Of the world outside.

Inside the cold walls of the habitat, she had not met any androids. But she *had* met some people who behaved robotically.

The wallscreen in front of her emitted light in phases perfectly timed to her circadian rhythm so she awoke with energy. Rubbing her eyes, she planted both feet on the floor.

How the alleged guards treated that poor girl in the cafeteria still did not sit well. The government had gone through a lot of trouble to ensure their survival. She understood the need for control, especially in an enclosed environment full of young adults and hormones. However, she disagreed with their methods.

There's so much going on here. Dad's message left on my necklace. Then Dexter being killed. Of course, that is probably just a rumor. But still. And this virus thing. It doesn't make sense. We all took the universal shot...

She slid her scrub shirt over her head and tightened the band around her scrub pants. Avalon touched her necklace and recalled her father's message before heading out to the cafeteria where she grabbed a granola bar on the go.

As she grabbed the plainly marked granola bar, she saw Elena. She recognized that platinum blonde hair anywhere. She had a hard angular face and thin lips. Combined with her heart shaped face, she should have been beautiful. And she was, but in the way that cut glass is beautiful. Or dry ice. Avalon didn't know how, but somehow the Accipio girls had managed to create makeup, because Elena's eyes sported thick black eyeliner and her lips were painted bright red.

A bit much, don't you think? Then again, we are the last humans on Earth.

Avalon looked around the cafeteria. She spotted some kinda hot guys, some not so hot guys, and a really hot guy—the one Ilium said was the President's son. She tried not to look at him dead-on, so she wouldn't be spotted.

He is definitely easy on the eyes.

Looking down at her watch, Avalon made a beeline on her way out of the cafeteria when Elena blocked her way. Avalon politely moved to the right, and Elena moved right. When Avalon turned to the left, Elena turned to the left. Elena's group of friends stood a few feet behind her scowling.

"Watch where you're going Fulcio," Elena said with a laugh.

Avalon rolled her eyes and turned to the left. Elena deliberately bumped her shoulder and knocked the granola bar out of Avalon's hands.

Avalon's face turned red as Elena and her gang of girls laughed.

Elena obviously wants a rise out of me. Probably wants the guards to come over and attack me.

"Stop," Avalon said.

"Stop," Elena mimicked.

"Please, grow up. I don't even know you," Avalon said.

"You don't have to know me. I know I don't like you," Elena admitted.

"Why? I haven't done anything to you."

"You don't have to," Elena giggled, her icy blue eyes like sharp knives and her teeth like a venomous snake.

"I don't want to start anything," Avalon said and stooped down to pick up the granola bar. But just as she stooped, Elena kicked it farther away.

Avalon balled her fists up.

"Hi, Elena, how is it going?" Kael said, coming up behind Elena. *No! Please don't be with someone like Elena.*

"Great, how about you?" Elena said in a different tone of voice than she had used with Avalon. It was almost awe-inspiring how quickly she could turn from venomous to sweet.

"Just the usual," Kael said as he led Elena and the gang of girls away from Avalon by telling some funny story. Somehow, Avalon didn't think it was a coincidence.

What the heck is her problem! Avalon picked up the granola bar and discreetly placed it back on the rack while grabbing another one that was less broken.

As she left the cafeteria, the standard issue black combat boots were a bit too big, and rubbed her skin raw, despite the socks she wore. It matched the growing irritation she felt at Elena. *Kael seems too dreamy…but then again I don't even know him! He could be mean.* But then she pictured his face and decided she didn't care how he was, if would just smile at her. *Girls like Elena always get guys like Kael. Who am I even kidding? I don't even belong in his world. What would we have in common?*

Avalon waved to her teammates as she entered the workstation and tried not to think so much about Elena, Kael, and the hundreds of questions on her mind after seeing the holographic message her father left.

Skylar strode over to where Avalon stood and said, "Today, I'm going to train you on how to use and analyze the systems. It is a huge responsibility and something we take very seriously. All of our survival is at stake, so I trust *you* will take this seriously as well."

Avalon nodded her head as Skylar continued, "Sometimes, it takes a minute for the system to become acclimated to how your particular neurons are configured." As Avalon stood upon the round circle on the floor, it emitted blue light as it read her biosignal and loaded up the training program.

"Welcome, Avalon," the AI spoke in a pleasant female voice.

After demonstrating to Avalon how to open folders and perform various operations for thirty minutes, Skylar left Avalon to her own devices.

"Once you complete the training mode, you will be able to work on the real stuff. Everyone has access to only certain areas of the mainframe," Skylar informed.

"Skylar," Avalon said.

"Yes?"

"Can you fill me in a bit more on everyone? Everyone seems so quiet."

"Xin is very serious and meticulous. He normally does not allow chatter," she said.

Avalon pouted.

Skylar rolled her eyes. "Ok, but it's gotta be brief."

Avalon gave a small smile.

"Xin's brain is wired in a way that is rivaled only by the highest artificial intelligence in his cognitive and analytical ability. He became the first human competitor to beat a machine at chess in over fifty years. He won *twice*, as the developers believed he cheated the first time."

"That's quite the achievement," Avalon answered.

Skylar nodded. "He is one of a kind."

That was the closest thing to a compliment Avalon had ever heard Skylar give someone on the team.

Then Skylar turned her head towards Brody.

"Brody is here because he worked with a professor to develop the trillion exoflops per second computer."

Avalon looked at Brody with new appreciation for his talents.

"And yours truly developed a pill with nanobots which could change your hair color, and I did it at age 14," Skylar said. "Women around the world could thank me for ending the hair dye industry. Now, all they had to do is pop a pill to stop grey hair." Then she frowned, "Of course, it only stayed on the market for two years before we had to come here."

"That's quite impressive," Avalon said.

Skylar smiled until she glimpsed Xin looking at her with his lips pressed hard together. "Well, I will let you practice doing it yourself," Skylar said as she returned to her blue workstation.

They must wonder what I did to warrant my presence. I am sure they just think I am only here because of my dad.

After a few hours of writing and executing code, the others took their fifteen minute breaks.

"Avalon you're a coding queen! Come take a break!" Brody yelled, seeing Avalon had reached 60% completion of her training mode already.

"I will soon, guys. I just want to finish training today and I will join you all afterwards!" she answered.

"Nobody finishes training in one day. It takes from three days to a week. Xin has the record at three days," Skylar added.

Avalon smiled and said, "Ok, thanks!"

Once the room cleared, Avalon sped up and blazed through the remaining training courses. She had slowed down in front of her teammates so as not to appear too smart. She had to work hard and fast so that people would respect the fact that she belonged on the habitat for her own merit—not just for her last name or connections. Yet, she didn't want to be so smart that she became isolated.

Despite her intentions, her name was now prominently displayed as number one on the training scoreboard, with completion in six hours.

There goes my popularity. O well. Might as well have some fun!

Avalon searched through files on her own and happened across a folder labeled Confidential. Normally, such folders would be restricted by biosignal. However, a small timer icon hovered next to the folder.

The timer represented how many minutes the President had left to secure the folder as being Confidential.

Avalon glanced over her shoulder. Biting the side of her bottom lip, she double tapped the folder. It looked like a video.

A male, roughly around age eighteen, appeared on the screen. The footage was from his helmet camera. *Why is he wearing a helmet?*

The short video continued to play. The young man in the suit said, "Yeah, there is nothing outside. Just this sea of red."

A second voice on the young man's ear comm said, "Just as we suspected. Area is a wasteland as predicted."

The young man sighed. "At least I got to go outside for a little while."

"True. But since there is nothing outside you're not to mention this to anyone, just as we agreed."

"Roger," the young man replied.

Then the young man walked around with a Geiger counter type apparatus the size of a small credit card. While the radiation levels were at levels too high to sustain plant or animal life, microbial life might have survived.

"Although, I don't understand why some of the stuff isn't here anymore. Like all of that razor wire and the big concrete wall when we entered the habitat," the young man said.

"I believe the sandstorms buried it," the voice on the other side said.

The young man nodded his head as he continued to walk, surveying the land using a map in his helmet.

"Everything just looks so different. Very similar, but somehow different."

"That is to be expected," the man on the other end said.

"I know. But I can't explain it. Something doesn't seem right."

"Perhaps, you should come on back then, son," the voice on the other end said.

The young man nodded.

"I think I will. My oxygen is getting low."

Right as the young man turned around to return, he saw something out of the corner of his eye.

"Hey....I think I saw something," the young man said.

"What?" the ear comm voice asked.

"I think I saw...a person..."

"Like you mean a face in the sand sort of thing?" the voice on the ear comm asked.

"No. I mean a person's face," the young man answered.

"You must be imagining things," the ear comm voice reassured him. "Maybe it's the radiation levels and different atmospheric pressure affecting you somehow despite your suit. Please return towards the habitat now," the voice commanded.

The young man pivoted and made a few steps towards the habitat. As he did, the footage shook.

"What the—" was the last thing he said before the video feed cut out.

The audio feed, however, remained. The young man screamed and cried. Then the audio feed ended as well.

What the heck was that? Did they run an expedition without telling anyone? And who is this young man? I don't recall seeing him in the habitat. He would have to be awake…

Avalon was still thinking when she was startled by the sound of chatter outside the door. Quickly, she snapped out of that folder and onto the current task at hand just as her colleagues returned. Her heart pounded as another person emerged from behind her teammates. Natural bronzed skin dressed in purple scrubs with a mop full of curly blonde hair could only be one person— *the President's son!*

Chapter Four

Avalon's mind raced as the President's son entered the room. *What is he doing here? Did he notice anything?* None of the scenarios her mind envisioned ended well.

"You finished training in a day!" Skylar shouted with astonishment.

"No— in six hours," Xin corrected with a tinge of jealousy.

"Are you a *prodigy?*" Brody asked.

Avalon smiled as Brody mispronounced the word prodigy. Brody provided much needed comic relief, often unintentionally. He had a kind, salt of the earth heart and polite manners. *With Brody hailing from a wealthy established family in Virginia, I wouldn't expect anything less.*

Skylar bristled at the compliments Avalon received.

Kael walked up to Avalon and extended his hand for a shake. "Don't be shy. My father has told me all about you."

Avalon had trouble listening to the words coming from his mouth as she connected with his outstretched palm. A warm sensation flew through her hand as her cheeks turned redder than the tomatoes she used to help her grandmother pick, distracting her from what she wanted to say.

"Allow me to introduce myself. My name is Kael," he said in his New England accent.

"Nice to meet you," Avalon said. *He may be an Accipio but he seems friendly. Of course, appearances can be deceiving.*

"I am conducting inspections, but I can see that everything is in good hands here. Keep up the good work," he said with a dimpled smile which sent a shiver through Avalon's spine.

With a wave and one last glance towards Avalon, Kael exited the room.

Skylar and Avalon sat in silence for a few moments before Skylar blurted out, "Can you believe he talked to you?"

Avalon just stood still and stared blankly.

"Ugh. You just don't know how lucky you are," Skylar said, staring off into space.

Avalon smiled remembering how he looked at her like she was the only girl in the room. Her face was still flushed as she took her lunch break. Her overprotective father ensured her inexperience with being the center of a boy's attention. So Avalon relished in the flutters in her stomach when she thought of Kael's smile.

Someone tapped Avalon on the shoulder as she stood in line to receive dinner that night. Avalon swirled her face around to see Ilium. As she smiled at Ilium, her gaze turned behind him to see where Kael sat. It did not take very long to spot those purple scrubs in the crowd. *There he is!* And then her smile turned into a slight pout as four buxom girls sat down next to him. *Figures. He can have any girl he wants—of course he wouldn't be interested in a Fulcio.*

"How did your first real day go?" Ilium asked.

Avalon snapped her attention back towards Ilium. She thought of telling him of Elena and that crowd but thought better of it. He could have had a bad day. No need to burden him with details.

"Well, I think it went pretty well. Thanks for asking."

"She's being shy," Brody said. Brody was a little bit ahead of them in line but still listening to their conversation.

"Really?" Ilium asked, glancing at Avalon with a simper.

"Yeah, she's fast as lightning man. She finished training in six hours," Brody said.

Ilium wore an expression of amusement mixed with admiration.

Avalon took a bite of her toast. It wasn't that bad. Then she looked at Ilium and decided to ask him a question which had been on her mind.

"Can you tell me some more about Dexter?"

"Sure," Ilium said. After he took a sip of his smoothie, "What do you want to know?"

"Well… what was he like?"

Ilium looked upwards as he remembered. "Cool kid. Quiet, smart."

Avalon nodded. "What did he look like?"

"Whoa now. I don't look at dudes that hard. I guess he was average height if that's what you mean," Ilium said.

"He had brown hair and brown eyes," Skylar added.

"Why do you ask?" Ilium asked looking at her intensely.

Avalon broke her eyes away and answered, "No reason in particular. Just curious."

I think Ilium knows more than he is letting on. But I won't press him in front of other people.

Instead, she sipped her water and surveyed the room.

A strange sense of unease washed over her. She looked to a table where Elena and Viggo sat.

Why is she talking to him?

All the quiet chatter in the cafeteria ceased. Avalon turned her head around. Six men entered the room wearing long purple robes. They were obviously members of the Council. But why would everyone stop their chattering?

The group of six moved in unison, and they stopped square in the middle of the cafeteria.

All six looked eerily alike. Their heads were shaved bald, and their eyes were icy grey.

"Yesterday a disturbance occurred in the cafeteria," the one in the middle announced.

No one moved.

"As you know, you are constantly being monitored, not only by the guards but also by cameras," he continued.

"We cannot have such dissonance and discord in such a small habitat. It will not be allowed."

All eyes were on the Council members.

"Those Compatios, or any of you really, would do well to know that those smartwatches attached to your wrist are more than fun pieces of metal which allow you to videomessage. They track you. And they cannot be removed."

As the one in the middle spoke, the other purple robed men stared blankly into the crowd.

They can't be removed? They didn't attach themselves to the skin. They weren't implants. I don't see how they couldn't be removed.

Avalon tugged against the watch to see if it would budge. After several attempts, it did not budge. The thing had formed a solid circle of metal, which could not be undone.

"They can also be used to inflict pain, should the need arise. We do not wish to utilize our influence this way, but as you all know peace must be maintained at all costs."

The other five robed men repeated the words, "at all costs."

Then the man in the middle decided to provide a demonstration of the power for good effect. A chorus of cries emitted from those in the Compatio sector.

"Consider that punishment for the disobedience of Michelle yesterday."

With a wave of his hand, the cries diluted. Blood trickled from the ears of the Compatio people. A signal from the smartwatch was sent to their ear comm, which had emitted a blaring loud noise.

"Consider this your warning. Farewell," the robed man in the middle said as the six of them sauntered out of the cafeteria.

Avalon, Brody, Ilium, and Skylar turned and looked at each other in shock.

"What the heck just happened?" Avalon asked no one in particular.

"Just grab your tray and sit down," Ilium told her. Avalon did as told and sat down at a table.

"Seriously. What was that?"

"We can't say much because everything they said is true."

Avalon leaned over to Ilium and whispered, "I was not aware this was a dictatorship or plutocracy. This was supposed to be a democracy."

Ilium did not answer her but instead sipped his smoothie. The others ate quietly as well.

"Did you know that the smartwatches had that capability?" she whispered.

Ilium subtly shook his head.

Avalon pivoted her gaze towards the table where the Compatio sector sat. All of them were in pain, holding napkins to their ears. Tears formed down their faces, but they dared not yell out.

"You're going to have a lot of patients in the morning," Avalon whispered to Ilium.

"Meet me later," he whispered back.

Avalon caught the hint and ate the rest of her meal in silence as she added Council to her list of things to avoid in the habitat.

Ilium and Avalon entered the storage room. Ilium memorized the hours that the janitors would visit the room. It was a relatively small place filled with shelves and tons of large cardboard and metal boxes. Robotic vacuums and other objects were spread around. One wall was made from the side of the mountain. His main reason for selecting it was that it was safe from the purview of the cameras.

"So, tell me what I want to know," Avalon said as soon as she entered.

"You're quick to get down to business aren't you?" Ilium smirked.

Ilium took a step towards her. "First, you tell me what you think you know."

Hm…he isn't dumb either.

"All of these rumors going around of Compatios coming down with a virus. Are they true?"

Ilium nodded.

"I knew it," Avalon said. "But how can that be?"

Ilium shook his head. "I don't know. I have a theory that it's related to the substances in their blood."

"What substances?" Avalon asked with alarm.

"Well, as a side project, I randomly collected some blood samples on people shortly after they woke up. It is totally unauthorized, and I could get in major trouble if anyone discovered I used precious resources like this—"

"They won't," she quickly reassured him.

Ilium let out a breath and then continued, "Well it turns out the Compatios have antibodies to a virus. A virus they should have been protected from via the universal shot. However, the shot doesn't cover this virus."

"Does it affect anyone else of a different sector?"

Ilium shook his head. "Not so far. I have only seen it in the blood of Compatios."

Avalon tried to calm herself. They were trapped in an enclosed space, with filtered and occasionally recirculated air. She was pretty sure it was in her imagination, but she felt the room was getting hotter by the minute.

"Is this virus deadly? How does it spread?" Avalon blurted out questions as fast as she could think them.

"The answer to the first question is it appears to be deadly. The answer to your other question is that I don't know how the virus spreads, or even if it does spread. I performed a rapid RNA and DNA sequencing of the virus using a cultured sample from their sputum. The sequencing perfectly matches across all four patients. All females from the Compatios sector."

Avalon sat down on a box in the corner. "A deadly virus. We haven't had anything like that in decades."

Ilium nodded. "Indeed."

"What could bring a virus like that back? In an enclosed space?"

"Now you're asking the right questions."

Avalon sat and pondered. "Sounds deliberate."

Ilium nodded his head in agreement. "Indeed."

Avalon rose up with balled fists to her side. "Who would do such a thing?"

"I don't know," Ilium replied.

"Why aren't all of the Compatios sick at once?" Avalon asked.

"I don't know. It could be, like the common cold, everyone who has exposure doesn't necessarily develop signs or symptoms."

Avalon chewed on a strand of her hair which had fallen loose from her ponytail. "Have you notified the President or the Council of any of this?"

"Just the President. I wouldn't go near the Council."

After the demonstration today, Avalon couldn't blame him.

"The President says to just keep him informed, as though there is nothing to worry about. However, he also told me not to tell anyone about the quarantine."

"Something doesn't sound right about that. For example, how do we find out who patient zero is? Or if we should quarantine them?"

"Who would deliberately infect the Compatios? And why?" Ilium asked.

Avalon wanted some more information on Dexter. And while they were sharing, she decided to share what she found out about Dexter going outside.

"No one ever mentioned someone going outside before," Ilium said as he struggled to take in everything.

"It was marked confidential. I am pretty sure no one was supposed to find out," Avalon said.

Ilium ran his hands through his hair.

"This is all just so crazy," Ilium said.

"Tell me about it," Avalon said.

Avalon looked down at her watch to read an incoming message.

"I am sorry, but I've got to go. Maybe we can meet tomorrow?" he asked.

Avalon nodded and she headed to the President's office.

Viggo spoke to someone on a secure and private line. His feet were propped up on his metal desk, but he quickly placed them down when he received the phone call.

"I don't know if I can do that, sir," Viggo said, spinning around on his lab chair.

After listening to the other party speak, Viggo nodded his head, straightened his back, and said, "Yes, yes. I understand exactly what is at stake."

After a pause, Viggo spoke again, "The results are less than stellar thus far." He lowered his gaze to his chart. "I know about the timeline," he said with a sigh.

"Yes, I am making progress. Although not as quickly as you liked."

Nodding his head, Viggo added, "I am being careful. No one—"

"Ok. I will be more careful next time."

Hanging up the phone, Viggo let out the breath he was holding on to as he scrutinized a large algorithm displayed on his wallscreen. A Rubik's cube sat on his metal lab desk, half solved.

Viggo closed his eyes and reflected upon his days conducting genetic experiments with food. Those were the days. Most of the developed nations stopped consuming genetically modified food, known colloquially as GMOs, decades ago. However, America still consumed them, and the corporations made record profits year after year. Some of which were used to line Viggo's pockets as well.

As a result of his prestigious accomplishments with GMOs and other genetic related fields, Viggo had been cherry picked for his position in the HOPE habitat after Mr. Adams could not board.

Viggo opened his eyes and held the Rubik's cube in his hand. As he tinkered with it, his mind continued to reflect back on that fateful day when the asteroid hit.

On that day, the day the asteroid struck, Viggo had placed all of the other members into their cryochambers.

Safe inside the HOPE habitat, the President, warned him against viewing the destruction of the world on the televised broadcasts. But Viggo insisted on seeing it live.

He figured he had a front row ticket to the end of the world.

He ordered the wallscreen to tune to WNN and WOLF news so he could receive coverage from both sides of the aisle.

WNN operated on a skeleton crew as most of the people were long gone to whatever meager shelter they had prepared for themselves. The cameraman included. Only one or two neurotic anchors who wanted to be immortalized for telling the news even in the face of death remained. *Who did they think would be left alive to care?*

WOLF news, on the other hand, had several news anchors still on the air as they were safe in underground bunkers. Safe was relative, as they lacked enough money for cryochambers, but they had enough food etcetera to last about ten years. The news anchors demonstrated how to use canned foods and MREs (Meals Ready to Eat) to survive. WOLF news had preached so-called "prepper planning" for decades.

Then it dawned on him. The Amish. They were a simple people. They might survive the impact even though they lived outside of the dome. But only if they moved underground. Yes, wholesome, unpretentious stock like that might survive.

Viggo watched the wallscreen as anchors on both WNN and WOLF turned their heads towards a loud sound.

The autocamera on the drone shook, and the male reporter for WNN was knocked to the ground. He still had his mike on and he announced that the event registered as a 9.5 on the Richter scale which was normally used to measure earthquake severity. Birds squawked and flew away in a desperate attempt to avoid destruction. Dogs barked on the streets, and armadillos and snakes emerged from their holes.

The male anchor, who had never before expressed any sort of religious inclination, fell to the ground and prayed just as glass was blown out and flew towards the camera. The station went dark.

Tears rolled down Viggo's cheeks.

WOLF news also had a camera drone on the outside while their news anchors watched the destruction in stunned silence. The asteroid tore through the sky, piercingly loud, bright, glowing, and fierce.

Viggo snapped out of his daydream, and said to the air, "I have a lot of work to do."

Chapter Five

*F*or *the President to message me, it could only mean one thing—I am in trouble.* Avalon swiped her wrist across the sensor to enter the large office suite whose décor was in stark contrast to all of the other rooms in the habitat. The off-white walls were decorated with ornate oil paintings. A simulated floor-to-ceiling window was dressed in long gold window coverings. On the mahogany desk, sat a few digital photo albums featuring a handsome young man with curly blonde hair at various ages. Audiobooks about history, psychology, biology, and military warfare stood at attention in the built-in bookcase alongside a marble bust of the President. Two long leather couches faced each other in the middle of the carpeted room.

The President stood in the middle of the room and urged Avalon to sit down on the couch.

She didn't want to, but the look in his eyes and his guards' faces let her know it was not a choice.

"Someone has accessed a file on our server marked Confidential. Since you're on the computer tech team, I thought I would ask you if you knew anything about it?"

Avalon tried not to sweat. She hated to lie, and worse, knew it was futile. How could she forget they constantly recorded everything in this place?

"That's good. You are silent. I prefer that to lying. You are very smart, Avalon, like your father."

Avalon hated the President mentioning her father. Each time he said the words, her heart ached.

"What are you going to do?" She asked, ready to get her punishment over with.

"Nothing my dear. Nothing at all. Because you never saw any videotape and it doesn't exist. Furthermore, you were never in my office. Do you understand?"

It takes a minute before I realize I won't be punished for accessing the file.

Avalon swallowed. "Yes, sir."

"Consider this a warning, Ms. Adams. Should there be a next time, I won't be so nice."

Avalon nodded.

"Good. I will have my guards escort you back to your room."

Avalon knew she should heed the President's warning and stop snooping around. Whoever was in the video did not matter anymore. But she could not give up so easily. The fact the President went through such lengths to prevent her from snooping again, meant the trail was warm. He was covering something up.

Stuff is happening so fast. I just woke up and I've learned I am all alone. All my friends and family are gone, the United States government as I knew it ceases to exist, there's a mysterious virus in the habitat, and I am the in the bullseye of the President.

A few days later, Avalon decided she needed to expand her horizons if she was ever going to find the answers she needed. That included talking to more people than her inner circle. She needed Kael. So she looked at the VR room schedule and chose the time that he normally blocked off just for himself.

"What brings you here?" Kael asked, with that brilliant smile of his as she entered the VR room. "I thought I booked alone time."

"Oh, I didn't mean to intrude. I've had a hard few days and I wanted to relax on the beach. I miss it," Avalon answered.

"I didn't know that. Why didn't you tell me? Is there something I can do? Call someone else in to lighten your load?" He flashed a smile.

"No, that won't be necessary. Thank you, though," Avalon said with her best smile. While she didn't have lipstick, she made sure to smear the strawberry smoothie across her lips to tint them a cherry red color. For her eyes, she burnt the tip of a kohl pencil and smeared a line beneath them. She also borrowed a friend's one size too small scrub shirt.

Kael couldn't keep his eyes off of her. "Mind if I join

you?" he asked.

Avalon smiled and nodded her head. *So far, so good.* Both of them stepped behind a curtain on opposite sides of the room to remove their scrubs and don a bodysuit and a leotard respectively. Both the bodysuit and leotard were specially fitted with levitation technology. Grabbing a handful of sensors each, they placed the stickers on their wrists and ankles.

"You ready?" he asked ogling at her mile long legs a moment too long.

"Sure," she answered biting the corner of her lower lip as his abdominal muscles poked through his bodysuit. His broad shoulders barely fit.

They each placed black VR goggles around their eyes and loaded the program. Immediately, Avalon was swimming in the middle of the ocean, inhaling the salty air, and listening to the sound of waves as they crashed around her. Seagulls flew in the crystal blue sky above, looking for fish to eat, and the bright orange sun cast a shimmery glow like diamonds on everything

She turned her head to face Kael who smiled at her with intense brown eyes, his blonde curls wet from the ocean water. The sensors picked up on his exact body profile and her pulse quickened as he stood in the water, showing off his six pack abs.

His skin is so flawless. Wait! What am I doing? I am on assignment. A mission. I can't be distracted.

"Nice huh?" he asked peering at her.

The corners of Avalon's lips turned upwards as she noticed how the blonde in his hair played off the golden flecks in his espresso eyes.

"It's uncanny how realistic everything looks," Avalon answered taking in his every feature. His angular jaw line, his pearly white teeth, and plump lips all combined on his perfectly symmetrical face. His muscles, solid like marble, betrayed his privileged status.

After a brief silence, he asked, "So how do you like the habitat so far?"

"It's ok. Although some things are hard to adjust to… like the Council," Avalon said.

Kael nodded. "I don't think we ever fully get used to it. It's just not normal, you know? For everything you know to disappear at once. But I am glad you're making friends so quickly."

"Come again?" Avalon asked.

"Your friends."

"You mean Ilium?"

"Yeah."

Friend. Ilium *was* her friend. It was next to impossible to have friends in a place with constant surveillance, but in a span of a few days, she felt very close to Ilium. But feeling close to someone meant you let your guard down, and she couldn't do that completely with anyone yet. Not even Ilium.

"Are you two….?" Kael asked.

Avalon raised her eyebrows. "A couple? No."

Kael chuckled and moved a little closer to her until their eyes were a mere six inches apart. His teeth were so white. Accipios must be using toothpaste with hydrogen peroxide, and not the plain stuff the lower levels received.

"Are you in a relationship?" Avalon asked.

"No, but I think anything is possible," he said while gingerly caressing the side of her face. Her eyes closed at his touch and warmth flooded her body.

He is off-limits. He is an Accipio, and would never date a Fulcio. I don't know who he thinks is playing. But if he wants to play a game, I can play along.

Avalon tried to focus on the seagulls squawking overhead. Tilting her head, she asked, "So who did you leave behind?"

"Excuse me?"

"Like pets, friends, etc. Pardon me if I am too direct."

"No. I just haven't met anyone as frank as you in the habitat. Most people are total brown-nosers."

Avalon chuckled, and Kael smiled.

"I left behind a dog."

Avalon frowned. She really hated that pets had to be left behind.

"Even the President's son wasn't allowed to break that rule. I also technically left behind a brother."

Avalon's eyes grew wide.

"Don't worry. He died five years prior to us entering the habitat." His eyes shifted upwards as he remembered. "He rode his cycle while drunk after a frat party." Then his eyes lowered to the ground. "Hit a tree going ninety miles per hour."

Avalon winced. "I'm sorry to hear that."

"Yeah," his gaze remained on the floor. "We've all

lost people."

Avalon nodded. She tried to fight back tears at the thought of the ones she had lost.

"The worst part is trying to fill his shoes," Kael said.

"Then don't."

"Come again?"

"Don't try to fill his shoes. Fill your own."

"Avalon Adams. That is the second pearl of wisdom you've given me. How much do I owe you for your gracious service?"

Avalon giggled.

Avalon looked into his face. "Kael, do you know anything about Dexter?"

"Yeah," he answered. "What do you wanna know?"

"Well. I just wanted to know what he looked like, things like that."

Kael crinkled his nose as he tried to remember. "He was average height, brown hair, brown eyes. Nice fella. Never saw him too much."

He sounded very convincing. And that description matched the young man she saw in the video.

"May I ask why you want to know about him?" Kael asked.

"Oh, no reason," Avalon said.

After a few more minutes of swimming and casual conversation, Avalon stepped out onto the beach. Her feet were like sandbags pulling her down into the sand. Avalon lay down on the beach shore, and Kael soon followed. The water beaded and glistened against his chest as he lay down beside her. Avalon removed her

VR glasses and ended the rendezvous.

"Thank you for joining," Avalon said.

"My pleasure," he said. "I hope we do this again sometime?"

"Sure," Avalon answered. Kael reached and grabbed her hand sending electricity through her body.

"Hey, there's a party tonight. Don't tell others as it's invitation only. Would you like to come?" Avalon thought it over. *I should really be working with Ilium on figuring out what's going on. But then again, I might be able to find something out there.*

"Yeah, where is it?"

"I'll videomessage you when the time comes," he said.

Avalon managed to find her way to the party. It was held in a small room which her smartwatch guided her to via a text Kael sent. The room was made out of rock on all four sides and clearly was never meant to actually be a room. It was more like a literal hole in the wall that they just found.

A bunch of alternative rock played so loud that her heart thumped in tune and goosebumps immediately formed on the hairs on the back of her neck. She could not see one foot in front of her, and everyone had a glow in the dark nitrogen filled concoction in their hands.

Couples made out on couches and in dark corners. Some girls and guys had dipped their hair in some glow in the dark solution. Some had glow in the dark streaks, others only had it on the very ends of their hair.

A slight smell of body odor lingered in the air as people sweated and gyrated and twisted to the music in such a cramped space.

They somehow managed to fit a pool table in the corner where some boys played pong with golf balls. A lot of people were losing, judging by the passed out bodies.

Some people were actually dancing on the dance floor, and before Avalon knew it, her own body moved and twisted to the beat.

Avalon locked eyes on Kael, but he didn't see her yet. It was easy to spot Kael in any crowd. He was the tallest and usually surrounded by a gang of either girls or guys. He had one of those personalities where he never met a stranger. He stood talking to another Accipio male. Avalon read their lips.

"Man, you haven't danced with a chick here. I know Elena isn't here, but that's all the more reason you should get with the *chicas*," a coffee hued Accipio said.

Kael chuckled.

Elena? So he did have a girlfriend! Of course, he would. He is rich and good looking. But did it have to be that snob?

"Don't tell me. Is it that Avalon chick? Man…if Elena ever finds out…"

Before Kael could answer, he spotted Avalon, who turned around to leave.

"Hey," Kael said as he ran up to catch her.

Avalon didn't answer, she didn't even bother slowing down or turning around.

But Kael managed to catch up with her as the crowd was thick and hard to cut through. Kael stood in front of her.

"You're beautiful," Kael said.

"As beautiful as Elena?" she asked.

Kael blushed. "I didn't mean for you to hear that. I am not dating her. She has a huge crush on me, yes, but I'm not dating her."

Avalon looked up into Kael's face. His intense eyes were staring into hers, and for some reason, she chose to believe him.

"Besides, you shouldn't eavesdrop on people," he chuckled. Something was different about this version of Kael. He was carefree, mischievous, and rogue.

Avalon looked around the room. "So, this is where you go to hang out."

Kael glanced sideways at the general crowd and then returned to face her. "Yeah. Helps us decompress."

"But you keep it hidden from anyone but Accipios?"

"Yes."

"Doesn't that seem elitist?"

Kael's head tilted as he deliberated on the matter. "I didn't consider it like that. I just felt like people enjoyed conversation best with like-minded people."

"Hm. It's kind of short-sighted of you, don't you think?"

Kael stuck his tongue in his cheek. He was so cute at times that it was hard to stay mad at him. But still, he had a lot to learn. As an Accipio, he never had to deal with the rations and true work that the Fulcios and Compatios dealt with on a daily basis. That was one of the blessings of his position—he never really had to think.

"You really have a way to make people feel good about themselves. Has anyone ever told you that before?"

Avalon gave a half-hearted smile. She scanned the room and noticed a bunch of girls were ogling Kael while others were scowling at her. While Kael was pretty oblivious to the scene around them, Avalon was quite aware.

"She shouldn't be here. She's that Fulcio girl," someone whispered.

Avalon was reminded that despite Kael's aloofness when it came to sociopolitical concerns, he was nicer than most of the other members of his class.

Then someone else caught her eye. They were watching her through a small space in the crowd. A shudder ran through her spine as she met their glare. Someone who looked a lot like...

"I need to go now," Avalon said.

"So soon?" Kael asked with furrowed brows.

"Yeah," Avalon said as some girls began dancing next to her. "Sorry!" Avalon said as she brushed past the girls and shimmied towards the door.

"Was it something I did?" Kael shouted.

Avalon paused and turned her head towards him. She shook her head, and continued moving towards the exit.

Avalon stood before the exit, but she was blocked by the Accipio Kael spoke to earlier.

"Wait— are you just gonna let her skip out on us like that?" he asked Kael.

Kael stepped up towards his friend. Kael stood a full six inches taller than him.

"I said she is good," Kael said without blinking.

A tension filled silence fell over the room. The music stopped playing. Everyone ceased dancing and stared at what was happening.

His friend, Ed, flared his nostrils in frustration.

Kael tensed his jaw. There was a look in his eyes Avalon had not seen before. An intensity. A dare.

Ed rolled his eyes and reluctantly stepped aside and let Avalon slip past.

Once Avalon reached her dorm, she showered and shampooed her hair. Closing her eyes in the shower, she reflected upon how the Accipios had their own secret space where they could decompress away from the watchful eyes of the cameras. There really wasn't much difference between them and the people in the Fulcio and Compatio sector. They weren't as vapid as they appeared either. The fact the Compatios were becoming ill wasn't lost to them. But the care, the concern, necessary to change things was missing. The curiosity which propelled her to seek answers. Of course, most people were like that. If it wasn't something that affected them directly, it didn't matter. Somehow she had to figure out a way to make it matter. To make it more than just the Compatios problem.

As she continued to scrub her scalp, thoughts of Kael flooded her mind. She remembered the feeling of electricity which raced through her veins, the feeling of warmth as she stood so close to him. And then her thoughts ran towards Ilium. *I've got to see how he is coming with everything. We must get together and compare notes.* Despite the awful situation of being without family in this concrete tomb, friends served as a vital palliative to the monotony and solemnity which surrounded each day.

Stepping out of the shower, Avalon yawned as she quickly towel-dried her hair just enough so it would not be damp as she slept. *I hate to run out like that on the party, but I was trying to catch that guy. He looked a lot like the guy on the video. But it can't be. That guy has to be long dead. Nobody could live after all that screaming. Could they?* Reaching into her drawer, she pulled out her pajamas and socks.

She waved her wrist across her bed pod, tired, and ready to step inside and fall fast asleep. Instead, she stood dead in her tracks, paralyzed.

Someone was lying in her bed.

Chapter Six

Every hair on Avalon's body stood on end as she tried to stifle a scream by quickly wrapping her hands around her mouth. Her heart beat out of her chest as her pulse rung in her ears. Her sense of sight heightened as she watched for the slightest twitch of movement. *Should I pull back the sheet? But then whoever is in there may wake up. Who is in my bed? And why?*

Avalon's gaze fell on the dorm door status. Locked displayed on the glass surface. Avalon was in the deep end of the ocean, alone, scared, and about to be pulled under. After several minutes of hesitation and watching the stranger not move, she had to take action. Her gaze darted around the dorm room, desperately searching for anything that could be used as a weapon. *Maybe it's just a sleepwalker. Maybe I am overthinking.* Finding nothing that could be used as protection, she took a deep breath and lifted the sheet from the lying form.

All of the blood drained from her face. The Compatio she helped earlier in the cafeteria was lying in her bed.

Except the girl no longer had a rosy glow behind her copper toned complexion. Her black spiral ringlets hung limply beside her more ashen face. Her chest did not rise and fall. She did not breathe. Avalon dared touch her to be sure. Cold. No mistake about it. She was *dead*.

Fear and adrenaline raced through Avalon's veins.

The room began to spin as Avalon tried to grab a hold of the cold, slippery metal walls for support.

Taking a big breath, Avalon struggled to get her thoughts together. *What should I do? Who should I tell? Kael…no…..Skylar…no…Brody….no…Ilium…yes…Ilium.*

Avalon swiped her wrist and ran all the way down to the boy's dorm.

She scanned her face in front of the camera intercom and dialed Ilium.

Ilium came outside to meet her, wiping sleep from his eyes. His hair was disheveled.

"What's wrong?" he asked with a yawn.

"Ilium…Ilium…"Avalon kept repeating, visibly shaking.

"Calm down. Take deep breaths," Ilium said rubbing her back.

"That girl…that girl…"

"What about a girl?"

"She....She...she's in my bed!" Avalon screamed.

"What girl is in your bed?" Ilium asked.

"That Compatio girl from the cafeteria!"

"Oh. You mean Michelle. That's great. Leo, her friend, has been looking for her."

Avalon shook her head. "No, you don't understand...she is dead!"

Ilium stood still. "Dead?"

Avalon nodded. "Dead."

Ilium's eyes widened as he leaned in closer. "Are you sure?"

"Yes!" Avalon screamed as her face grew hot.

"Ok," Ilium said as he ran his hand through his hair causing it to spike a little. "Calm down," he said, placing a hand on her shoulder. "Take me to your dorm and I will see how to handle this."

Avalon ran down the corridor with Ilium in tow.

Swiping her hand over her dorm room door, she yanked Ilium inside.

"See!" she pointed frantically to her bed capsule.

Ilium gazed at the girl whose chest did not rise. Whose eyes did not flutter. Who was pale blue, lying in Avalon's pod.

He grabbed Michelle's ice cold wrist. "Ok," he said after letting it go. "She *is* dead."

"I know that," Avalon said with a hint of irritation in her voice. "Now what do we do about it?"

"Well," Ilium said, scratching his hair. "I want to know how she died first."

"That is a good question. But, *I* want to know how she got here so I won't be next."

Ilium stood in silence, trying to gather his thoughts.

"Ok. Here is what we are going to do," he finally said. "We are going to tell the guards that somehow Michelle is in your bed, and she is dead."

"Gee, that sounds well and all, but what if they think *I* killed her?"

"Nonsense!" Ilium replied.

"How did she even get here? I thought I was the only one who could open the door to my dorm?" Avalon said, slumping down onto the floor.

"You're supposed to be the only one. I don't know how they did it, besides hacking," Ilium answered as he slid down next to her.

Avalon searched her memories. Michelle had mentioned abductions earlier. Maybe someone had figured out a way to hack the doors in order to abduct people at night. And Michelle was the latest victim.

Ilium regarded Michelle's body. "There's no blood," he said in a calm voice.

"Ok," Avalon said. "What does that mean?"

"It means," Ilium said, "That I don't think she died violently."

"Ok…" Avalon said stretching out the syllables.

Ilium stood up and pointed to some sores. "Look at these odd sores and marks on her body, though."

Avalon rose up to look and began to gag.

"I can't look anymore. I *just* want her gone!"

"Ok. But let's take a minute to think about this calmly. This girl does not appear to have died a violent death. She has sores on her body consistent with radiation exposure."

"Radiation?"

"Yes."

Avalon tried to hold it together.

"How would she get that much exposure?" Avalon asked.

"I don't know, other than going outside."

Avalon let that information sink in. She remembered the video she saw of Dexter leaving the habitat and the President and Council not informing anyone of that.

"Someone probably forced her to go outside."

"But who would do that? And why?" Ilium asked.

"They would do it to see if it's all right for us to go outside yet."

"But the countdown clock clearly shows we aren't ready."

"Whoever did this didn't care about a clock."

"Do you think it was as a punishment? For her outburst in the cafeteria?" Ilium asked.

Avalon shook her head. "I don't know what to think. All I know is that I am freaking out because there is a dead body in my room, and I don't know how she got here nor who put her here. How do I know I am not next?"

"All right, you must not go down that lane. Just breathe."

"You're always saying just breathe and be calm Ilium. But we can't just breathe and be calm all of the time!" Avalon yelled.

"You're right," Ilium said. "But I don't know the answer to your questions. What I am worried about right now is how much radiation her body is currently giving off."

Avalon made a beeline for the door when Ilium caught her by the arm.

"Let me go! We have got to get out of here!" she yelled.

Ilium held on tight. "Wait. I know I said I am worried, but we have already been exposed. I am not letting you go until we think this through. Clearly, someone planted her body here. If you just go, who's to say you didn't kill her?"

Avalon's eyes grew wide. She hadn't thought of that.

"But you said it was radiation. I couldn't kill her with radiation?"

"Yes, that is what *I* said. But what I say doesn't matter. Haven't you already seen that?"

It was true. Avalon remembered the Council and everything that had occurred in the habitat. The Council's version of the truth was the version that mattered.

"So what do we do then?" Avalon said. "I am not going to just sit here and meditate?"

"I am going to message for the guards. They will take care of everything."

"But Ilium! What if the guards are part of it?"

Ilium shook his head. "I doubt that."

"But what if they are?"

Ilium sat and thought for a minute.

"I can't think of anything else to do right now. But the guards were not chosen for their intelligence. They were chosen for their brute strength. Whoever orchestrated this possessed intelligence."

Avalon nodded and took a deep breath.

Tears rolled down her face. "What is going on Ilium?"

Ilium wrapped his arms around her and held on tight. He patted her hair as he whispered, "I don't know. But we are going to get through this ok?"

Is this the danger Dad somehow tried to warn me about?

Ilium dialed the guards using videomessage on his smartwatch.

"Yes, guards? I need you to come to Avalon's dorm, Room 58—"

The guard didn't see the rest of the videomessage, because they were plunged into total darkness.

Chapter Seven

Avalon let out a bloodcurdling scream while Ilium rushed to cover her mouth in the darkness.

"Calm down! I am sure it's something electrical. The generator has to kick on in exactly sixty seconds. You know this."

Avalon stopped screaming and became limp against Ilium's body.

"It's going to be ok. As soon as the lights return, I am going to finish the videomessage," Ilium said.

Avalon nodded her head.

Ilium continued to hold Avalon close to him in the dark. Ilium's chest rose and fell against her skin, and as she listened to his heartbeat in the dark, it comforted her. A few seconds later the lights flickered back to life, just as Ilium said they would.

"Told you," he said. Avalon looked into his empathetic eyes and tried to concentrate on his soothing voice.

"Call them now!" she yelled.

Ilium dialed them.

"Guards. Yes. There is a situation in room 589 and we need you to come right away."

"What is it?" the guards asked.

"I am going to show you. Brace yourselves," Ilium said as he moved towards Avalon's pod.

Avalon gasped.

The sheets were perfectly folded and tucked under with no sign a human body ever touched it. For a second, Ilium and Avalon both stood frozen, too surprised to move or speak. Avalon's body turned numb.

"I don't see anything. Is this some kind of sick prank?" the guard said. "This is a waste of resources, which counts as two strikes."

"No sir," Ilium answered, an expression of shock and horror still etched across his face. "This was not a prank. We are very sorry. It may be a side effect of the sleeping pills I gave Avalon."

Smooth move, Ilium.

"Don't let it happen again or we will report it to the Council," the guard said before signing off.

Avalon and Ilium sat and stared at each other in silence. Ilium's face was a ghastly pale shade. Avalon's skin felt cold and damp. Both of them were thinking the same thing.

"What the frack just happened?" Avalon whispered.

"I don't know," Ilium said as he chewed on his lower lip. She could see the cogs of the wheel turning in his mind.

"I mean we saw that right? That wasn't just something we hallucinated together?"

"We definitely saw a dead girl's body disappear," Ilium answered.

Avalon and Ilium stood together in silence, taking in the sound of every breath between them. Then Ilium spoke. "Somebody took her when the lights were off."

"But, I didn't hear anyone enter the room. Did you?"

"No."

"Is there a trapdoor here?" Avalon asked, feeling around the smooth surface of the ceiling and floor, not finding any hollow or uneven surface. Avalon's mind continued to run wild, struggling to figure out how a body could just appear and then disappear when Ilium grabbed her arm and pulled her closer to him.

"I don't feel safe sleeping here," Avalon admitted struggling to hold tears in.

The truth was she never truly felt safe. While she enjoyed the peace and quiet of having her own space, it also got eerily quiet at night. The surroundings were all new and strange, and she didn't really count any girl on board as a friend. The President's threat didn't help either. She was constantly under low-grade stress, and her eyes were beginning to grow bags under them.

"I understand that. I am going to get Raleigh to sleep with you tonight."

"But. Who is Raleigh? And what do I tell her?" Avalon asked her voice faint.

"She is a close friend. You won't have to tell her anything." Ilium answered. "Let me handle it. Just make sure you call me first thing in the morning when you wake up, you understand?"

Avalon nodded.

Ilium locked eyes with Avalon and said, "I need you to say yes." *Ilium is taking this whole dead girl in my bed thing way better than me. But then again, the dead girl is in my room and not his.*

Avalon replied, "Yes, I understand." Something fluttered in her stomach, but she could not discern what it was with all of the insanity of the night.

Fifteen minutes after Ilium left, Raleigh arrived.

"I am really glad you came," Avalon said trying to hide her nervousness about the whole situation.

"It's no problem. Ilium said you needed someone to stay with you to settle your nerves. I am glad to be of help."

Avalon smiled. *She seems so sweet and genuine.*

"This old place can start to wear on a girl. Especially with you being in this dorm alone."

"Right," Avalon answered.

"I mean there is nothing to do here. Sometimes I go for a run through the habitat, but it's not the same as running outside."

Avalon nodded. She missed the outside too. Even having a real window with fresh air circulating. The way the sun's rays would hit her and warm her face. Birds chirping, nothing but clear skies above.

Raleigh glimpsed around the room. "You haven't decorated your room much."

"No, I haven't. Do the other girls do that?"

"Yeah. We just you know. Take a few materials here and there and make do. Like my roommate, Gen, knows origami. So we have tons of swans and dolphins in all different colors hanging from the ceiling and sitting on the dressers."

The other girls must have more free time or get really bored.

"That's really creative!"

"Yeah, she even made some storage boxes."

Avalon wished she and Raleigh had gotten to know each other earlier. Under different circumstances, Raleigh might have been a great friend. Someone that could offer a different perspective than Ilium.

"You think you guys could help decorate my room sometime?"

"Sure!" Raleigh said. "You know. This place isn't so bad once you get used to it. It beats some of the other places I've had to live." That was followed by a brief silence as she tilted her head to the side.

"Ilium wouldn't tell me exactly what happened or why you wanted me to come here. Can I ask, is there anything in particular?"

Avalon wanted to trust Raleigh, but it was just too soon.

Be careful who you trust.

"All of the silence can get to you after a while. I mean besides the comforting and ever-present background hum of electrical equipment."

Raleigh chuckled at Avalon's remark.

"So what made you willing to come here? Besides Ilium asking you to?" Avalon asked.

"He's my friend. He's a really good guy. Don't tell anyone but sometimes he shares extra medicine with people who need it."

Avalon nodded her head. Ilium was someone who would go the extra mile to help others. Most people in the habitat were more self-absorbed, but Ilium actually cared. The only one she trusted in the habitat.

Wait trusted? Dad said be careful who you trust. But…Ilium is different.

"Has anyone ever told you that you're really easy to talk to?" Raleigh asked.

Avalon shook her head and smiled weakly.

"Well, it's kind of getting late. If you don't mind, I am going to close this lid and go to bed," Raleigh said.

Avalon minded. She did not want Raleigh to stop jabbering. The jabbering filled the air with noise and kept her awake.

She didn't mean to pry, but she had to keep her chatting.

"If you don't mind my asking, where did you live before coming here?"

Raleigh looked at Avalon for a minute, sizing her up before answering.

"I am not as affluent as some of the others. My parents ended up taking on more debt than they could handle. Eventually, the house went into foreclosure. At first, bouncing around from hotel to hotel seemed fun, like an adventure. But eventually it got old."

Avalon could only imagine.

Raleigh could read her face. "Don't feel sorry for me! I turned out perfectly fine I would say! Unlike most of you all who bemoan all of the more fancy parts of life, I am just thankful to be in here alive. Anything extra— is just that extra."

Avalon was impressed with Raleigh's positive attitude.

Closing the lid, Raleigh plopped some earbuds into her ears and it wasn't long before she drifted off to sleep.

Avalon laid down wide awake in a different capsule, staring at the door and at Raleigh. Avalon envied how quickly sleep descended upon Raleigh, how oblivious she was to whatever had just occurred in this room. Perhaps, she looked *too* serene. *After all, I don't even know this girl. But no, she is Ilium's friend.*

Several more suspects swirled around in Avalon's mind as she struggled to stay awake and not succumb to the heavy fog of sleepiness pushing down on her eyelids. However, sleep won the battle and her eyelids shut.

Avalon dreamt she was back home in her bed with her dad making breakfast downstairs. How she missed the changing of the seasons, the feel of the warm sun on her skin, the whistle of wind through the trees. The smell of real food as it wafted through the house. Real buttermilk pancakes with sorghum syrup, poached eggs, and fresh orange juice. She looked out of the bay window on a crisp fall morning as the wispy white clouds rolled by the bright blue sky, her father sipping his piping hot coffee at the breakfast table while reading the latest news on his iPad.

Just as she reached out to turn her father around, she was knocked down as the whole Earth shook. A brilliant white light blinded her.

Avalon began screaming.

Raleigh shook her. "Avalon! Avalon!"

Avalon woke up to see Raleigh hovering near her face.

"Are you all right?" she asked.

Avalon panted as sweat trickled from her face. "Yes. Just a nightmare."

"It's okay. We all have them. It was about the asteroid wasn't it?"

Avalon nodded her head.

"We are gonna make it," Raleigh said.

Avalon wanted to believe Raleigh's comforting words, but the fact that Raleigh was in her room meant that last night was real. That a dead girl's body was in her room.

"Is it anything you want to share?" Raleigh asked.

"I'm good, thanks," Avalon answered.

Raleigh was not convinced.

"Thanks for keeping me company!" Avalon said.

"Sure. No problem. As soon as I remember who you remind me of, I will let you know also," Raleigh said as she left to go grab breakfast.

Avalon took the quickest shower of her life and got dressed in a rush. A million questions bounced around in her head and were about to burst from the seams. Once dressed, she videomessaged Ilium.

"Hey, how did you sleep last night?" Ilium asked.

Avalon had bloodshot eyes but she answered, "As well as could be expected. Did last night really happen? Please tell me it was a nightmare."

"I wish I could," Ilium answered, running his hands through his hair.

Avalon became queasy again. After taking a moment to calm her nerves, she said, "Something isn't right here. Who would do such a thing! And why? Why was I singled out?"

"I don't know. But I have to report to work. See you in the usual spot."

Avalon nodded her head and logged off of her videomessage.

To her surprise, as she opened her door, Ilium stood there.

"What are you here for?" she smiled.

"What do you think? Someone has to make sure you make it to your workstation safely," he said.

Avalon smirked to herself and enjoyed walking next to Ilium, despite the circumstances.

"Lay low. I want you to be safe," he whispered to her.

"Trust me. I want the same."

After a few steps, they stood before the doors of the Computer Systems room. "Thank you, my gallant knight," Avalon said as she entered the room.

"You're more than welcome, my fair lady," Ilium said as he bowed and rolled his eyes.

"Some people just can't help themselves, I guess," Skylar commented to Xin as Avalon walked up to her blue circle.

Avalon ignored Skylar's jealous comment and managed to keep calm, despite the hundreds of questions swarming like locusts within her. *Can I trust anyone besides Ilium?* Then she remembered the message her father left her. *No—I can't tell anyone else.* Everyone else could still be a suspect, no matter how unlikely. Even if they weren't directly responsible for Michelle's death, the person responsible more than likely had to have an accomplice to help drag the body into the room.

She continued to mull over everything, including the strange markings on Michelle's body. They looked like tally marks or a bar code... *What could it be?*

Avalon stopped in the middle of her work queue and grabbed her tablet.

"What are you doing?" Skylar asked as Xin continued to work.

"Just let me do this for a second!" Avalon yelled.

Skylar backed down but not before adding, "This *will* count against your scheduled break time."

Avalon continued to draw the marks down on paper. *These marks…they are a pattern. Wait! It is so obvious. It is Morse code! She just drew it in a circle!*

The code spelled out the letters H E L P M E.

Chapter Eight

Avalon stood dead in her tracks. Help me. A cry for help. *What did Michelle need help from? Who was harming her? And why?*

Avalon continued to think when the door opened and her head turned to see who entered the room. She recognized those blonde curls anywhere.

"To what do we owe the pleasure?" Skylar asked, quickly stepping in front of Avalon to greet Kael.

"I would like to speak with Avalon," he said, glancing past Skylar and towards Avalon.

Skylar's face turned several shades of crimson as she stepped aside. Kael's hands were behind his back.

"Good morning," Avalon said trying to ignore the excitement in her chest.

Kael smiled. "It's actually towards lunch time. I just thought that you have been doing such a good job with the habitat, that you deserved a reward."

Skylar's mouth fell open as Kael revealed a purple package which he handed to Avalon.

"Thank you," Avalon said as her heart beat a little harder. Carefully, she opened the cardboard box to reveal a bowl full of real fruits—apples, oranges, and even kiwi. She quickly closed the lid on the box, not wanting anyone else to see. *No Fulcio has had food like this since entering the habitat. They don't even serve these to the Accipios in the cafeteria. How did he get these?*

"Try not to eat it all at once," he said with a wink.

"Thank you so much," Avalon said as he stepped towards the door.

Avalon could feel Skylar's stares. "What did you get?" Skylar asked.

"Some fruit. Would you like some?" Avalon said. Perhaps, she could win her over by sharing.

"Fruit! How in the world did you get fruit?" Skylar asked.

"Is it real?" Xin asked. Avalon wasn't even aware Xin paid attention to anything besides the monitors.

"Yeah, it looks real. You all come grab some fruit."

Skylar greedily tore open the purple box and grabbed a Fuji apple. Voraciously, she bit into it and licked her lips without as much as a thank you.

Xin didn't even look at the box. "It's your gift. You enjoy it."

Avalon smiled at Xin.

"It's lunch time anyway," he said glancing up at the clock. As the others ushered out of the room, Avalon stayed behind and quickly changed the access codes to her room. Breathing a sigh of relief once it was done, her thoughts floated to the gift Kael gave her. *Why did he do that? Does he like me? Or is this some sort of trap. Could he be the killer?*

Avalon texted Ilium to meet her that night in the storage room.

"So, how was Skylar?" Ilium asked, twisting his lips into a smirk as he leaned against the wall of the storage room.

Avalon shrugged. "She was Skylar. Moody, kind of quiet."

"Ehh…Wouldn't expect anything less."

Avalon looked at his face anxiously, searching his eyes. *I wonder if I should mention Kael's visit to him.* "Well, are we any closer to finding out who killed Michelle? Or put her in my room?"

"No," Ilium said, shaking his head. "What makes you think she was killed?"

"Oh, I don't know. The fact her body just randomly appeared in my bed one day, and then it disappeared," Avalon said, with a roll of her eyes.

"You have beautiful eyes," Ilium said.

Avalon was thrown off guard but managed to stammer, "Thanks." The atmosphere in the small storage room changed. So Avalon decided to talk some more to break the awkwardness.

"I suspect the guards killed her. They could have done it to get rid of a perceived troublemaker. Or maybe the President."

"But why?" Ilium asked, moving closer to her.

"I don't know," Avalon conceded. "But I figured out what those weird markings were. A code. It spelled H E L P M E."

"That doesn't sound good," Ilium said with a grim expression as he sat down on top of one of the metal boxes and rested his chin against his folded arm.

"All of this is too much of a coincidence. The lower class Compatios are made weak with hard work and fewer rations, so obviously they can't rise up against the higher ups like the Accipios or the Council," Avalon said, as she folded her arms over her chest.

"And the rest of us are kept ignorant of what is going on outside the HOPE habitat. The President tells us that all of the drones we were supposed to send out for expeditions were somehow wiped out due to the high altitude electromagnetic pulse. Even though they were supposed to be specially shielded against such."

The room fell silent as both Avalon and Ilium contemplated what Ilium just uttered. The words reverberated in her skull and concentrated in her bones.

Avalon hesitated a moment. *How much can I trust Ilium?* They had been through a lot together. He really was the only one she had associated with most after hours. "My father left me a necklace that plays holographic messages. But he only left one message which erased after playing."

Ilium listened.

"The message said not to trust anyone."

"Sounds like he suspected something even back then," Ilium said.

"Do you know why he would say that?" Avalon asked.

"No," Ilium said genuinely. "But we can find out."

"You mean you're willing to help me?" Avalon said, eyes wide.

"Of course," Ilium answered.

A smile formed on Avalon's face.

"Ok. First, I will see what I can do with my access to some of the computer systems," Avalon said.

"Sounds like a plan," Ilium answered.

Ilium leaned forward and wrapped his arms around her. Avalon's back stiffened, unsure of how to react to this gesture. However, after everything they had gone through together, Avalon nuzzled her head into his shoulder and returned his hug. Avalon's pulse quickened and her body warmed up as she inhaled the scent of his hair and of his skin, which were so fresh, in contrast to their stale air surroundings. He mussed her long hair between his fingers. When they released each other, they both had a rosy glow.

"Ok, let me see what I can do," she smiled as she left the storage room.

The next morning, loud protestations from Avalon's stomach woke her up before the wallscreen did. She quickly swung her legs out of her bed pod and began to get ready for the day ahead. However, as she got dressed, she paused in front of the mirror for a minute. Her cheeks were hollowed, her features sharper and more defined.

After getting dressed, she ran past Ilium in the hallway on her way to the cafeteria. As he waved, her stomach fluttered.

That's odd. No. No. No. This can't be happening. Not here. I don't have time for anything more than friendship in this place. I have already lost so much.

Avalon grabbed a protein bar for herself and some cups of coffee for the team.

"Thanks!" everyone said, except Skylar, who politely declined as she did not drink coffee.

While in the process of working, Avalon's mind continued to think about Ilium. How he was the first face she saw when she woke up. How soothing his voice was, and how he smelled like lemons.

But at times, when he thought no one was looking, she could see sadness behind his blue eyes.

Once the shift ended, Avalon stayed behind, carefully grabbing Xin's cup after he dropped it into the recycling bin.

Avalon waited till the curfew for being in the dorm room had come and passed. At around 2300 hours, Avalon kicked the covers off of her and jumped to the floor. She leaned her ear up against the door. Silence. She unlocked her door via wrist swipe. Pausing, she turned her head left and right before crossing over into the corridor. As Avalon shimmied down the corridor, she checked over her shoulder every so often to ensure no one followed her. She also checked the halls for security cameras and tried to avoid being detected by them. The main rectangular shaped fluorescent lights were turned off to conserve energy, and only a few bare emergency bulbs lit the path. Under cover of darkness, Avalon reached the computer room. Sweat materialized on her armpits and her heart beat sped up. Avalon quickly swiped her wrist across the door sensor of the computer room and silently slipped inside.

Avalon stepped onto her circle, and the blue light illuminated her face in the darkness.

Carefully, she placed Xin's coffee cup on his login pad and stood on it, providing the necessary pressure for activation.

"Welcome Xin," the AI said.

Yes!

Trying to emulate Xin's voice, Avalon said, "Blow up Research files."

The Research files folder blew up. Going through several folder headers, she came across one named Code BK Max.

Hmm. That sounds interesting.

"Show details," she said.

"Access denied."

"Darn!" she said. *What could the Accipios be hiding? And who does have access?*

Several folders displayed, including one labeled Contingency plan. But she was short on time. So instead, she asked the computer a question related to her waking up.

"Computer, please play the video from when I awoke."

"Yes," the computer answered as it instantly brought up footage. Avalon enjoyed being nostalgic. However, as it played, she noticed something.

Avalon tilted her head to the right and asked, "Computer, please rewind the video ten minutes prior to me waking."

The computer rewound the tape. The video did not include sound, but Ilium could be seen walking around the infirmary attending to his patients. He moved slowly like he was tired, but he was very attentive to his patients, constantly checking their stats. About eight minutes into the video, Ilium exited the room.

Two minutes later, someone entered the room. This person pressed a ton of buttons on Avalon's chamber and shortly thereafter, the room was bathed in red lights.

Did someone cause my cryochamber to open prematurely? I could have died!

"Computer, zoom in on frame 10, 8:21 seconds please."

The computer attempted to zoom, but uncharacteristically, the image froze mid-zoom.

This was highly unusual.

Avalon scrunched her forehead and asked, "Computer, are you feeling OK?"

"Yes. I think I may need a quick reboot. I apologize for the freezing. Please wait fifteen seconds for me to reboot."

Avalon's stomach knotted as she waited for the computer to reboot. *Hurry, hurry, hurry!*

Her heart sank as the doors to the computer lab opened. She thought she had been listening, but obviously, she didn't listen hard enough.

Guess this is it.

Then the shadowy figure which entered the room stepped into the path of light.

"Ilium!" Breathing a sigh of relief, she whispered, "You scared me half to death. You aren't supposed to be here!"

"Neither are you," he said with a smirk. "But, I wanted to talk to you and I figured you would be here after our last conversation."

Ilium walked over to her and asked, "Well, did you find anything?"

"Yeah. Something about genetic modification and Code BK Max. Does any of that ring a bell?"

Ilium shook his head. "Nope. Can't say it does."

"My freaking cryochambers opening was no accident either."

"Are you sure?"

"Yes." She nodded. "It was deliberate. I watched video footage of a shadowy figure entering the room shortly after you exited. The figure pressed a series of buttons outside of my chamber after which my pod opened."

"So what you're saying is someone tried to kill you?"

The words "tried to kill you" kept playing over and over in her head along with thoughts of her father's warning. She never felt more alone than now.

Avalon's brow furrowed. "I don't know. But it sure seems like it. If you had not been there to rescue me, I would have died."

Ilium nodded his head and grabbed her hand. "I was there to rescue you though. And I always will be."

A smile crept across her lips, as she didn't feel so lonely anymore.

"We'll get to the bottom of this. Don't worry," he said gently stroking the side of her face with his thumb.

While Avalon wasn't sure of her feelings towards Ilium, she felt grateful for his friendship and affection.

Another thought came to Ilium's attention as she tried to separate her hand from his. He looked down into her face. "Let's assume this person didn't want to kill you for a minute. Why else would they unplug your chamber?"

Avalon paused. It was just like Ilium to explore all angles, never leaving a stone unturned.

Avalon shrugged. "I don't know. But obviously, you have something in mind."

Ilium nodded. The way he looked at her could become problematic. His fingers tightened around hers, causing her stomach to have unwelcome sensations.

"Someone could have wanted you awake now instead of later."

Chapter Nine

Fragmented images haunted Avalon that night. Her nightmare did not start off that way. At first, she dreamt of the world outside. She held someone's hand as the wind washed over her face. But then her friends began choking. *Why were they choking? What were they choking on?*

Avalon startled awake. Her hair was matted on her face as she had sweated profusely. As her heart rate returned to normal, Avalon kicked the sheets off her bed and hurriedly got dressed for the day.

Avalon returned to her work station and her teammates. While there, she reflected on how she came to enter the habitat in the first place.

The government pretended to hold a lottery for a slot in the habitat to keep the peace in the streets. The trick to the lottery was that anything could disqualify you— from traffic violations to littering. If you made the lottery cuts, the next step was to participate in a series of tests. What the public was not privy to was that the 5,000 people were largely pre-chosen from birth. This preselection was mainly based upon genetics. Those pre-chosen went through the motions of taking tests, but as long as they passed the psychological and physical tests, they were pretty much-assured entry.

Interestingly, the world population stopped growing and began to reverse in the decade before the asteroid hit. Some conspiracy theories said it must be chemicals the government placed in the water. Others said the government created climate change through seeding the clouds and causing some areas to experience drought while other parts of the country were expecting too much rainfall which led to flooding. In some states, it was a crime to collect rainwater, a natural resource from God. These rules were actually enforced by "water police" who could issue citations and even place you in jail for a few days. The water issue got so bad that some people burst open fire hydrants for fresh water.

Of course, as far as America was concerned, people had long stopped believing in something the Boomer and Millennial generations described as the "American dream." It was basic enough—a house, two or three kids, two cars, and a TV and laptop per person. While most people had the technology part, very few owned homes. Homes were only for the rich. And the middle class continued to erode while only the lower and upper classes blossomed. The wealth of the upper class grew exponentially, and the traditional ways of entering via meritocracy, i.e. entrepreneurship or university attendance, all but dissipated.

In those last days, those who were rich enough began hiding in their shelters. Of course, if they lacked a cryochamber or other mechanisms besides canned foods to survive, they wouldn't last very long. The affluent, which were also intelligent, maintained a low profile and drove luxury armored vehicles. Others weren't so lucky. When the panic began, several people were left dead as others broke into their shelters. Sometimes in their haste, the trespassers permanently damaged the very shelter they took by force.

Someone waved a hand in front of Avalon's face, bringing her back to reality.

"Earth to Avalon," Skylar said.

"Hey," Avalon said.

Skylar rolled her eyes. "Viggo is here to see you."

"Viggo?" Avalon asked.

"Yes. Viggo," Skylar pointed to Viggo, who stood near the door.

Avalon cautiously walked up to Viggo. She hadn't seen him in person since she woke up. Sure, her father worked with him and he had been over to the house, and he appeared to be a nice guy then. *But why now? Why care about me so much now?*

Viggo wore his trademark black-rimmed glasses which barely covered the dark circles underneath his eyes. He was a bit lankier than Avalon remembered, and his hair showed a few signs of gray around the temples though the majority was still a dark shade of brown.

"Hey," Avalon said like it was a question.

"Hey," Viggo responded, concern in his eyes. "I'm so sorry I haven't had a chance to see how you were doing. I have just been so busy with everything."

Avalon remained silent.

"Your father charged me with helping to watch over you. I hear you're very successful, which doesn't surprise me. I didn't expect anything less from Avalon Adams," he added with a smile that didn't quite reach his eyes.

Avalon nodded. While it was like her father to assign a guardian over her, she wasn't sure Viggo would have been her first choice. He was always kind of absentminded, no matter how brilliant he was at science. "Thank you," Avalon muttered.

Viggo peered over her head and into the computer lab and then back at her. "Listen, can we step outside for a moment? I want to chat with you for a few minutes."

Avalon glanced over her shoulder at Xin, who nodded and said, "Five minutes."

Viggo walked along the corridor with Avalon. "Now how are you *really* doing?" he asked.

"I'm okay," she said.

"I'm not trying to be nosey," he said readjusting his glasses onto the bridge of his nose. "It's just that there have been some strange occurrences happening."

Yes! He sees it too.

"Like what? I haven't noticed anything strange." *Play it cool. Let him reveal information to you.*

"Now, Avalon. You're too intelligent for that. There is no need to fib to me. You're telling me you haven't noticed several of the Compatios becoming sick?"

Avalon nodded.

"I am worried about you," Viggo said as he placed one hand on top of her shoulder.

"But I'm not a Compatio. So why would you be worried about me?"

"I always worry about you. Remember? I've been entrusted with your safety."

Avalon looked at Viggo. She just couldn't believe her father would place *him* over her. Viggo had definitely changed under the confines of the habitat. He looked like he hadn't slept in ages.

"When was the last time you got some sleep?" she asked.

Viggo chuckled. "How nice of you to be concerned with *me*. I am fine."

Avalon's nose crinkled. "If you've noticed the Compatios turning sick, why haven't you alerted the Council or the President?"

"Oh, I have," Viggo said. "They know all about it. But they don't want to create alarm throughout the habitat, so we are trying to keep everything quiet."

Avalon studied his face. Viggo had said her father asked him to watch over her. But he also said to trust no one.

"I really should go back." Avalon gestured towards the Computer center. "I think it has been five minutes."

"All right," Viggo said, obviously a bit crestfallen. He placed a hand on her shoulder. She bristled under his touch.

Cool it.

"But if you ever need me, you know you can call anytime." He gave another smile which didn't quite reach his eyes.

As much as I would love to have an adult on our side during this investigation thing, there is something about Viggo. But he did work with Dad…maybe I can trust him?

Avalon smiled faintly and waved before returning to the computer lab.

<hr/>

At lunch time, Avalon sat by Ilium at the end of a long table. Skylar and the rest of the team waved at them from the opposite end of the table.

"Do you think Skylar or anyone is suspicious of us sitting here alone?" Avalon asked.

Ilium shrugged and said, "Who cares."

A flush formed across her face. Avalon bit off a piece of fruit and asked, "So what else have you discovered?"

Looking around from side to side and lowering his voice, Ilium answered, "Well, the universal shot we received has two different effects. If you're an Accipio or a Fulcio, there are no ill effects. However, if you're a

Compatio, there's a high probability that you will become sick, although not immediately."

"So, that could be what happened to Michelle? She was a Compatio."

Ilium nodded his head in agreement.

"Also sounds like there could be two different universal shots," Avalon whispered.

Ilium nodded and took a sip of water.

Avalon split open her potato and wished desperately that they could have afforded cows for butter. She poured the two rationed packets of pepper and salt into it and mashed it all together before taking a bite. "We still don't know who planted her body in my room, or why. It is someone in this habitat, though. It scares me that we don't know who."

Ilium wrapped an arm around her. "Don't worry, I won't let anything happen to you."

Avalon flushed at the thought of Ilium being protective of her. "Thank you," she said and took a sip of water. She thought she caught a glimpse of a spark in his eyes. His voice was definitely huskier when he said he wouldn't let anything happen to her.

Avalon continued to eat. After a while, she lowered her voice to a whisper. "I feel like this virus thing is taking over our whole lives. We don't really talk about much else," Avalon said.

"Yeah, but what else is there really to talk about?"

Good point.

"I don't know. Like who is dating who or something?"

Ilium chuckled. "You have the wrong guy if you want that sort of thing. If my head isn't bent over a microscope or a patient I am not of much use."

Avalon smiled. As she continued to eat, she noticed Viggo out of the corner of her eyes.

"Hey is that—" she began.

"Is that who?" Ilium asked.

But just as soon as she said that he was gone. She lost track of him amongst the crowd of people moving back and forth.

"Never mind," she answered. Something about Viggo made her feel uneasy, but she couldn't pinpoint what. He worked with her father, so he should have made her feel comforted. Familiar. But something felt…off.

Avalon chewed on her boiled egg. "I ran into Viggo earlier today."

"The scientist?" Ilium asked as he took a bite of his salad.

"In the flesh. You know he and my dad worked together back in the day."

Ilium nodded as he took a sip of his water. "What did he want?"

"I don't know. He acted kind of peculiar. Said a bunch of stuff about Compatios becoming sick and him being worried about me."

"That's really weird. I mean for him to start off the first conversation he has had with you in goodness knows how long that way. Especially since you aren't a Compatio."

"Exactly," Avalon said. Then she took a bite of her food. She thought she was becoming used to the blandness of the food.

"Do you think he knows more than he is letting on?" Ilium asked.

Before Avalon could answer that question, Kael stole her attention as he walked towards them.

"Hey! What are you up to?" Kael asked Avalon.

"I'm fine. How about you?" Avalon said.

"Good, I guess. Do you want to visit the rec room today?"

"No, not today. Maybe later this week?" she replied. Heat radiated from Ilium as he stared daggers at Kael. The gaze wasn't lost on Kael, who analyzed the situation, noting Ilium's arm around Avalon's waist.

"Ok," Kael answered as his lips formed a tight line. He turned and walked away.

"What was that all about?" Ilium asked, irritation obvious in his voice.

"Nothing." Avalon smiled. "Jealous much?"

"Not jealous. Just wondering if there is anything between you too."

"No," Avalon answered, taking another bite of her potato.

"Then why is Elena staring at you?" Ilium asked.

Avalon checked out the faces sitting around the Accipio table. Surely enough, Elena's ice blue eyes were boring into Avalon like a laser through steel.

"I don't know…" Avalon said. *Kael didn't say he had a girlfriend. Although I am sure plenty of girls are naturally interested in him. He is the most eligible bachelor around after all.*

"But for some reason, I don't think he would mind if something was between us," Avalon said.

Ilium took another bite into his lettuce and tomato salad, chewing it a bit longer than he usually did.

"Besides, by hanging out with an Accipio I may get some more clues," Avalon added.

Ilium had to admit she was right, although he kept the thought to himself. He scowled at the back of Kael's head for the rest of the meal.

"Just promise me you will be careful. I don't trust him," Ilium said.

"I don't think you trust any guy that much," Avalon said.

"What is that supposed to mean?" Ilium said with harshness in his voice.

"Nothing," Avalon said.

"You can do what you want. Date who you want. I am just saying he is his father's son. Make of that what you wish," Ilium retorted.

Avalon did not care for the cavalier attitude Ilium displayed as he said date who you want. She didn't know why, but she far preferred when he was jealous.

"Just meet me tonight in the storage room so we can discuss this some more," Avalon said before leaving. Despite his efforts not to, Ilium watched the graceful sway of Avalon's hips as she walked away from him.

At around 2000 hours that night, Ilium met Avalon in the cluttered storage room. Avalon shivered in the corner, her lips turning a shade of purplish blue.

"You're cold," he said.

"I will be ok," she answered, teeth chattering.

Ilium took his shirt off and handed it to her.

Avalon took in the sight. Despite lacking six pack abdominals, he wasn't exactly flabby. His defined muscles were on a slim body. Avalon quickly slid the shirt over her head.

"Thanks," she said with a smile. Then she found a nearby storage box and sat down.

"So, interviewing people yielded some interesting results. Turns out, word amongst the Compatios is that there is someone who doles out extra rations and points as long as you follow him. No one knows who this person is, and no one sees people after they choose to follow him or her."

"So, why would they continue to go?" Avalon asked.

"Because they are starving," Ilium answered. "Starvation has interesting effects on the human brain."

Avalon mulled over what he said. "I've been thinking about what you said. I think that the universal shot must be triggering something in the Compatios."

Ilium leaned forward. "I agree with your hypothesis. Once triggered, the virus appears to do more than just make them sick. It appears to change them. At a cellular level."

"That doesn't sound too good." Avalon said with a frown. "What is it doing exactly?"

"It appears to be enhancing certain elements of their genome. Genes which control things like strength and intelligence and immunity. But the process looks downright painful."

"So it's a beneficial virus then?"

"Apparently. If one survives the process," he said.

Avalon knew it was completely the wrong time to do so, but she could not help but to gaze into his eyes. He held her gaze, and again her gaze fell to his slender torso and she bit her bottom lip.

Focus!

"Why are we even trying to fix this thing then?" Avalon asked as she leaned forward and rested her elbows on her knees.

"Because everyone doesn't survive the process," Ilium answered as he placed the shirt back over his head.

Avalon stood up. "Then I really think we should blow the top off this thing and let others know."

"No," he said, eyes full of worry. "You won't reveal anything."

She hated how Ilium would make statements like that.

"Why not?"

"Because I won't let you endanger yourself."

It was hard to argue with someone who always had your best interest in mind. Yet, she couldn't abandon the rest of the crew.

Avalon sat back down. "But everyone deserves to know."

Ilium scooped down and placed his chin on top of her head. Avalon closed her eyes and inhaled his scent.

"Let me handle this. We don't have enough information right now."

Avalon did not always agree with Ilium. It was difficult to keep all this information between them and not share it when other people's lives were at stake. While she understood Ilium's rationale, it still seemed wrong to keep this information to themselves. In the end, she trusted Ilium and his guidance.

"Ok, but only if you promise we will reveal this thing once we do," Avalon said with a sigh of frustration. Then she removed his shirt and tossed it back to him.

"You sure you don't what to keep it?" he smiled.

Avalon's heart fluttered as her gaze fell on his lips.

Shaking her head, she answered, "If you walk around shirtless, there will be questions. So no thanks." But there was a twinkle in her eye.

"See you later, Sherlock," Ilium said with a smile.

Then Avalon removed his shirt and threw it back at him.

"Why are we trying to fix this thing then?" Avalon asked as she leaned forward and rested her elbows on her knees.

"Because everyone doesn't survive the process," Ilium answered as he placed the shirt back over his head.

"I really think we should blow the top off this thing and let others know," Avalon said.

"No," he said, eyes full of worry. "You won't reveal anything."

"Why not?"

"Because I won't let you endanger yourself."

"But everyone deserves to know!" Avalon said.

Ilium scooped down and placed his chin on top of her head. Avalon closed her eyes and inhaled his scent.

"Let me handle this. We don't have enough information right now."

Avalon did not always agree with Ilium. It was hard not sharing this information with everyone. She understood Ilium's rationale, but it seemed wrong to keep this information to themselves. Still, she trusted Ilium and his guidance.

"Ok, but only if you promise we'll reveal this thing once we do," Avalon said with a sigh of frustration. Then she removed his shirt and tossed it back to him.

"You sure you don't what to keep it?" he smiled.

"If you walk around shirtless, there will be questions. So no thanks," she answered. But there was a twinkle in her eye.

"See you later, Sherlock," Ilium said with a smile.

That night Avalon reflected upon all the events which had transpired, as she struggled to distill and synthesize the truckload of information that was thrown at her over the course of a few days. Michelle's body was there one minute and gone the next. Compatios were sick with a virus they should have been protected from. A virus which if it didn't kill you would make you stronger, faster, and smarter. Yet it wasn't communicable because the members of the Fulcio and Accipio sectors were not catching it. A young man had already ventured outside before, but the government deliberately kept this information hidden from citizens.

This whole thing must be bigger than one person—it sounded like an orchestrated series of events. *Who was working together to this end and why?* No matter what question she asked, it all circled back to the same conclusion. She was trapped inside this habitat— with a killer.

Chapter Ten

The image of Michelle's dead body lying in her dorm and disappearing did not leave Avalon.

Before she found Michelle's body, Avalon believed there was a chance she could lay low, do what was asked of her, and perhaps make it outside alive. Now, everything had changed.

Yet, Avalon could not reveal to the others her true emotions. She did not know who she could trust, besides Ilium, so it was safest to trust no one.

Day after day, Avalon diligently searched and looked for clues, careful not to leave a trail. Her keywords included, "how to activate a virus, how to create a retrovirus, trigger for retrovirus, virus promoter, etc." These terms pulled up about 656,000 articles per keyword, so it took some time to sift the wheat from the chaff. Many a night she fell asleep with the wallscreen still displaying search results.

Days began to take on a pattern. Work, eat and meet with Ilium. Her day to day job consisted of running full diagnostics on systems to ensure everything worked properly. Systems included things like the airlocks, oxygenator, air filters, water storage units, and backup power generator. If a system had problems, it was logged into her work queue.

Ilium stopped by every night and checked on her. Sometimes they played old-fashioned card games into the wee hours. Other times they held each other as they whispered about what they missed from life before. Once he was assured she was all right and nothing out of the ordinary was happening, he returned to his dorm.

But one night he was late checking on Avalon. And then the walls in the dorm felt like they were tightening around her. Avalon kept her composure, and as soon as Ilium buzzed her door, she let out a sigh of relief.

"Sorry, I was late today. Had a bunch of paperwork and stuff to finish," he said with a flushed face as he had run to her room.

But Avalon didn't care about hearing why he was late. She was just grateful that he was here now.

But she also hated how much she had grown dependent on Ilium. And in such a short time span. What used to be something he did as a courtesy, she came to see as mandatory.

"Don't worry about it. You're here now," Avalon said, staring into his sky blue eyes. A shiver ran through her.

What is it about Ilium? He is perfectly ordinary. He is not wealthy, or the President's son. He isn't exactly exciting. He's risk averse. And yet…

He stepped closer and rubbed the back of his hand against Avalon's face.

"As long as I'm here, you don't have to be afraid. I don't know exactly what is happening in the habitat, but it will have to go through me to get to you."

Avalon stepped towards Ilium. His face moved towards hers. Her pulse quickened, but Ilium stopped short of meeting lips at the sound of his smartwatch beeping.

He frowned as he checked the message.

"Anything wrong?" Avalon asked.

"No, I just need to check on something later," Ilium said. His jaw clenched tight, however.

Avalon frowned, but let him go.

"You would tell me if something was wrong, right?" Avalon asked.

Ilium smiled before saying, "I have to go. I will check on you again tomorrow. Buzz me if you need anything."

Ilium stared into his microscope. He adjusted the light and the magnification levels.

"This can't be good," he said to himself.

He heard his door open and stood frozen. The person stepped into the light. It was Brody.

"Hey! What are you doing?" Ilium asked.

"Just wandering around the building. I thought you might want one of these cookies," Brody asked.

"Cookies? How on earth did you get cookies?"

"I don't know. Somebody just left a box of them outside my door. I didn't ask questions. All I knew was there was something sugary besides those fruit smoothies."

Ilium crinkled his nose. "What kind are they?"

"Chocolate."

"I didn't know we had chocolate in the habitat. Sounds too rich for my blood. How did *you* get some?"

"Man. Don't look a gift horse in the mouth."

"But doesn't that bother you? That you're eating something that you don't where it comes from?"

"Look, I didn't come here for the third degree. I am just going around the habitat offering people some cookies cause I know how hard life can be in this place. If you don't want any, that's fine."

"I'm sorry. I would take one, but I am busy at the moment."

"I understand. You sure you don't want one for later?"

"I'm sure," Ilium said with a forced smile.

"Suit yourself," Brody said, taking another bite of the delicious cookie.

As Brody walked out, Ilium relaxed. His eyes returned to his microscope with a furrowed brow.

A few days later when Avalon woke up, displayed across the wallscreen was a message from the President.

"Today is day one of survival training. It will commence at 1800 hours and end at 2000. It will be required once a week."

Guards led Avalon and the group to a new much larger room. The room corresponded to the one Avalon saw in the blueprints when she went snooping. Her stomach instantly tightened. There were several different centers—including one with a cardboard target on the wall, one with agricultural skills, and one for tent-making.

Avalon headed straight for the gun center and picked up a small six-shooter.

"Why do we need guns?" Avalon asked.

"Well, most things were destroyed in the cataclysm, but we aren't sure about smaller animals. Always better safe than sorry," the instructor said.

"They would have mutated, though, right?"

"Probably."

Avalon's hand shook as she grabbed the gun. Avalon had never held a firearm before. The smooth metal felt cold in her hand.

"Don't worry. It's rubber bullets," the instructor added.

The instructor stood behind Avalon and told her to use both hands to hold it by the handle while pulling back the trigger. At first, the trigger was hard to pull, but finally, the gun fired. The recoil startled Avalon as her eyes closed briefly at the loud noise the shot made.

When she opened them, she had missed the red circles on the target completely.

The instructor shook his head. "Never close your eyes. Better luck next time."

The noise from the gun's firing still rung in her ears.

"Maybe I would have done better with earmuffs?"

"In the wild, you won't be wearing earmuffs. You need to get used to shooting a gun, feeling the recoil, and enjoying the noise."

Ilium walked up and confidently picked up a .380 handgun. Without hesitation, he fired and hit the target dead in the center.

"Great job!" the instructor said.

"How'd you learn to fire like that?" Avalon asked.

"I'm from the Midwest, remember? It's what we do. Hunt and fish."

Humph. Makes sense.

"But, you were in an orphanage? So how did you get access to a gun?"

"I didn't enter the orphanage until age nine. My Dad had taught me how to shoot by then. Small things like squirrels and such. But I was always accurate."

Avalon wanted to ask more questions, but loud applause startled her. As she turned her head, Elena had fired a gun with deadly precision as well. Elena smiled her snake-like smile at Avalon.

Scanning the crowd, Avalon noticed Brody was absent.

"Have you seen Brody?" she asked Ilium.

"No."

Everyone has to report to this. It is mandatory.

Panic began to swell in Avalon's chest.

"Time to move to agriculture," the instructor said.

As Avalon and Ilium were ushered towards agriculture, Avalon continued to scan the crowd in search of Brody. She barely heard the instructor speak about how to plant the seeds, and water them, etc. All the seeds in the habitat were organic so they could save and re-use the seeds to produce new plants. It was quite elementary stuff, but still important to go over.

The next day, as Avalon signed in, she noticed Brody was not there.

"Where is Brody?" Avalon asked.

"He stayed in bed today. Said he had a cold," Xin said.

A cold. Avalon began to panic. *No. It has to be just a cold. Surely it can't be the virus.*

Still, as panic rose in Avalon, she could not concentrate on her work queue. She videomessaged Ilium to meet her in the storage room.

"So, how is it going with the virus?" Avalon asked once they were in the storage room.

"Not so good," he said.

"What do you mean, not so good? Maybe now is the time we should warn the others?" Avalon asked.

He fell quiet as he contemplated the answer. He looked at Avalon for several seconds.

Ilium shook his head. "No, not yet. I don't want to cause alarm if it's unwarranted." Ilium answered.

"Well, what have you found out?" Avalon asked, crossing her arms in front of her. "I can tell by your answer you know something."

Ilium let out a puff of air. "It's mutating."

Avalon's eyes grew wide. "Mutating…into what?"

"I don't know. But it is mutating, and I believe it now has the capacity to infect us all."

Avalon sat down. "This changes everything."

"I know. My original hypothesis was that the universal shot the Compatios received upon waking up from the cryochambers contained a retrovirus. While the one the Accipios and Fulcios received did not contain this retrovirus. So I believed the other classes weren't in danger."

"Ilium. Brody didn't show up to work today. Do you think—?" Avalon couldn't finish the words.

Ilium patted her on the back. "No, I don't think so. It is probably just a cold."

"But if he does have the virus…we cannot afford to lose him. Or anyone else for that matter," Avalon remarked.

"I know."

Tears formed in the corners of Avalon's eyes, stinging them. Her thick lashes clumped together as her lips trembled. Avalon tried wiping them away with the back of her hand.

"I've been working non-stop on trying to fix this," Ilium said, placing one hand on her shoulder.

Some of the tension melted from Avalon as she held his gaze. He moved his hand from her shoulder and placed his arm around her waist, moving her in for a side hug.

Her tears stopped their flow as he gave her a real hug. His heart was beating fast, and her eyes closed.

"A girl as beautiful as you should never cry," he said, looking down into her face.

Avalon's eyes met Ilium's and a silence grew between them. It was not awkward, like most silences.

"Do you think the Council is behind this?" Avalon asked, cutting through the silence.

"I'm not sure," Ilium answered. "I definitely believe the President is involved."

Avalon gritted her teeth. "We can stop him. Together. But this is teamwork. I can't do it alone," Avalon said. "I need your help."

"You have my help," Ilium answered. "I think we have come as far as we can with the knowledge we currently possess. We need more data on the immunologic biometrics."

"So, how do you propose we get that?" Avalon asked.

"I don't know. But I think the answer is in Viggo's lab," Ilium said.

"Why his lab? Viggo hasn't done anything to us. Besides, he worked with my father. My father handpicked him."

"Who else could orchestrate these events?"

Viggo's lab was the logical place that the virus would have originated. But she hoped it wasn't him.

"Anyone. The President. The Council. But I refuse to believe Viggo has anything to do with this."

"I think you're blinded," Ilium remarked.

"Blinded by what?" Avalon asked.

"The desperate attempt to hold onto anything related to your father."

Avalon's eyes stung and her face turned red.

"I didn't mean it like that," Ilium said trying to grab Avalon's arm. She jerked away.

"Listen, I take it back. I only meant we need to look at everyone. We can't be biased. Remember what your father said. Trust no one," Ilium stated.

Avalon took in a deep breath and calmed down. "Well, if we need to enter his lab, we'll need to break in," Avalon answered.

Ilium looked like he was about to choke on something. "Do you mean *trespass?*"

"Yes. Trespassing should be the least of your worries with all we have been through. I don't have a way to trick the system with his biosignal. So we only have one way in."

Chapter Eleven

Later that night, Ilium and Avalon entered a huge room full of microscopes and lab equipment. "Are we sure about this?" Ilium asked as they entered.

"Yes," Avalon replied. She had mentally calculated the odds of being caught, and what to do if they were countless times. She was ready.

Ilium tried to distract himself from the carousel of ways they could get caught, what might happen to them if they were caught, and more. Ilium's life was normally very planned and did not feature many adventures or anything dangerous. Life in the orphanage where he grew up was very scheduled, military-like in its regimen. *What would my life have been like if I had grown up with a family?* He didn't care if the family was poor or rich, or middle class. Young or old. All he wanted was special people to hug and laugh with and share memories with—to do things that weren't set to a time limit. All of a sudden, with the addition of Avalon, spontaneity was quickly becoming his new best friend. Furthermore, he was feeling a connection which was more than friendship. His heart beat raced and warmth spread throughout his body whenever she was near or he heard the pleasant sound of her voice.

"Whoa. We have a huge comic book fan," Avalon whispered as a section of wall was littered in various comic book pages. No one read comics on real dead trees anymore, and those pages would have been worth millions before they entered the habitat.

She found everything highly organized—pipettes, pipette tips, test tubes, were all neatly tucked away and labeled. Beakers, well plates, cylinders, Petri dishes all sat neatly upon the table top. Her fingers brushed against a bottle labeled Acetonitrile in one of the drawers.

It reminded Avalon of chemistry and biology labs in high school—of that one kid who almost set his face on fire by lighting methanol. Class was canceled the rest of the day. She headed home in the new electric car her parents had just bought her for her sixteenth birthday. It was top of the line and ran from solar energy. Sometimes she would set it in manual and drive it herself, but other times she liked to enjoy the autonomous feature while she closed her eyes and slept or read a magazine.

Ilium searched inside a side closet, but quickly closed it, having found nothing suspicious.

"It was just me and my dad against the world. We were a team," Avalon added.

Ilium bristled as he had always wanted a family like that. A team. A unique and special connection with someone.

"I don't think we are going to find anything," Ilium whispered as his hands ran across the smooth walls searching for anything suspicious.

"We must continue to try. Something has to be here." Ilium bumped the wallscreen.

"Hey! He hasn't logged off yet!" Ilium whispered.

The feeling in the room immediately changed.

"He just made this so easy!" Avalon whispered.

"What's this already on the screen?" Ilium asked.

A folder called Contingency plan displayed. Double tapping it Avalon read the following:

Harper Majors, age 18. Received 10 ccs of serum. Survived radiation exposure level for 30 minutes. Convulsed and died 2 days later.

Annabelle Atkins, age 22. Received 100 ccs of serum. Survived radiation exposure level for 60 minutes. Convulsed and died 4 days later.

Michelle Clue, age 20. Received 1000 ccs of serum. Survived radiation exposure level for five days. Patient exhibited improved breathing capabilities in carbon dioxide rich environment and improved strength and speed for Days 2-4. Died of unknown causes on Day 5.

Avalon and Ilium's faces glowed under the blue light from the hologram as they read the case files.

"What are we looking at?" Ilium asked in horror.

"They are Compatios. These are the ones that the rumors said were abducted."

"Michelle!" Ilium said.

"It sure is," Avalon said. "And all of these people are female."

"But what, what was Viggo doing to them?" Ilium asked.

Avalon studied the screen a minute before answering. "It appears he was trying to build a race of radiation proof humans."

"Unsuccessfully," Ilium said, looking at the death count.

"My question is…why? This is unlike the man my father described and who occasionally came over to the house to discuss work."

"Maybe he isn't doing it willingly. Maybe he is doing it for someone else," Ilium said.

Avalon shook her head. "His morals are too high for that."

"Maybe his morals *used* to be too high for that."

Avalon sighed. People changed. But still, she had to hold out hope that some things remained the same.

"I have a different problem," Ilium whispered. "These charts show people are dying. So where is he hiding the bodies?"

Avalon's eyes widened as she and Ilium exchanged a look of terror.

At that moment, Avalon gasped at the sound of footsteps approaching. Quickly, Avalon and Ilium turned off the lights and ran inside of the side closet. Ilium crouched in front of Avalon, protecting her. Avalon found herself grabbing hold of Ilium from behind and trying not to breathe too loud.

They listened as Viggo entered the room. Avalon's heart thumped against her chest as she held her breath. Ilium placed one arm around her waist and held her tightly. Her eyes closed, and she began to think less about her fear of Viggo, and more about the slow rise and fall of Ilium's chest.

Viggo stood a few feet away from them, and only the flimsy door separated the two. *Did I return everything to its place? Does he suspect anything?*

Avalon strained to listen by placing her ear to the door. Drawers opened and shut. Then her attention focused on how close she was to Ilium as they crouched together in the dark. It was a small closet. Her whole life was a series of being stuck in one box or another. But this box, here with Ilium, wasn't so bad. Still, every time she listened to Viggo's footsteps, her heart beat faster. Ilium somehow sensed her adrenaline rush, and he wrapped his arms around her even tighter. A few funky smells wafted into the closet, but after a while, they heard the sound of Viggo leaving the lab again.

Breathing a sigh of relief, Ilium whispered: "I'm going to step outside."

Avalon shook her head. "What if he only stepped out for a minute?"

"True. But we don't know how long he will take. It's a gamble."

Although Ilium could not see Avalon's face, he sensed her hesitation.

"I will crack the door open first," he said.

"Ok," Avalon said.

Ilium carefully cracked open the door. No signs of movement. He crawled out and remained crouched inside the lab. Once confirmed clear, Avalon followed him outside of the closet and into the main corridor.

Together outside of the lab, they stole away to her room without looking back.

"I can't believe we got away with it!" Avalon said breathlessly once they were inside her room.

"I can't believe we did it either," Ilium said.

Avalon let out a puff of air. Ilium stepped towards Avalon, gazing into her brilliant eyes which still held onto innocence in a habitat which didn't deserve her presence. Like a flower growing in a desert, she did not belong and required constant vigilance and protection, even if she did not realize it.

Ilium took another step towards her and held her gaze. With one arm, he pulled her close. Avalon closed her eyes and enjoyed the electricity which flowed between them until, without warning, Ilium took a step back. Avalon opened her eyes and looked at him. His cheeks were red.

"Now that we know that's he's experimenting on people, what do we plan to do with this information?" Ilium asked.

Avalon liked the sound of the word 'we' from his lips. It wasn't the first time he had used the pronoun, but this time it seemed to hold more promise.

"We've got to find a cure,"

Ilium nodded his head in agreement before the two parted ways. Avalon collapsed to her bed with her clothes still on.

The next day Avalon entered the workstation and noticed one floor circle was unlit.

"Is Brody still sick?" Avalon asked.

"Yes," Xin said.

Avalon immediately left and hiked down the long twisting corridor walking towards the infirmary.

This has to be more than the common cold for Brody to miss another day. For each day he misses, he receives fewer ration points for food. Ilium assured me it was just the cold.

As she entered the room, there were seven people lying in beds, and the stench of sickness hung like a thick cloud in the air. Avalon's stomach churned as patients vomited and coughed.

Out of all the patients lying on their backs in the tiny metallic trolley beds, not a single Accipio was amongst them.

Ilium stood in the middle of the room, giving one of the patients water.

"How is Brody?" Avalon asked.

Ilium shook his head. "I'm sorry Avalon. It turns out he does have the virus."

Avalon did not allow tears to form. She was developing thicker skin by the day. Tears would not help this situation. Action had to be taken.

"How close are we to something? A fix?" Avalon asked.

His grip tightened around the stethoscope in his hands. "I've been working on a formula non-stop, but I can't make it work. At this rate, it only delays the inevitable for a few days, but it's far from a cure."

Avalon took a deep breath to clear her mind. *I came here to check on Brody.* She strode over to him. Large black bruises were underneath his eyes.

"Hey. How are you doing?" Avalon asked.

"Just beautiful," Brody said with a cough and a half smile.

Avalon gently petted his sweat drenched hair and her voice cracked as she said, "You're strong. You're going to survive this. We all are."

Brody nodded. "I don't know what's going on. We all got the universal shot so none of us should be sick."

Avalon exchanged a look with Ilium. "Maybe the shot isn't so universal," she answered, too softly for him to hear.

Brody coughed. "Sure are a lot of us here. Nobody dies from this right? After a day or two, I'm going to get better?"

His chest rose and fell with great effort.

"Get some rest," she said, ignoring his question.

"You know, I would have thought those other cads would have visited me. Seeing as we see each other all of the time. But this illness has shown me who my real friends are," he said between coughing fits.

Avalon patted him on his shoulder. "Everyone loves you. Don't you worry about anything except getting better," she whispered as he began to fall asleep from the medicines entering his IV line.

Avalon plodded back over to Ilium before she let out the sadness she was holding in.

"Do you think we should tell him the truth of his prognosis?" she asked, lower lip trembling.

Ilium shook his head. "We can't. We can't do anything but work on the cure."

"Isn't that inconsiderate? He has a right to know that he may die," Avalon replied.

"Why? If he is going to die, what good does it do to tell him?" Ilium countered.

Avalon conceded he had a point after a long beat of silence. The decision still left her feeling uneasy.

Ilium handed her a microchip. "Maybe you can play with the formula?"

"I don't know anything about biology. I'm into computer science."

"Just try for me. You recognize patterns. Perhaps, you can see something I don't see."

Avalon nodded her head as she placed the microchip in her shirt pocket and returned to work.

Avalon inserted the microchip Ilium gave her into a small slot in her bed capsule later that night. She began toying with the computer model determined to figure something out. She could not let Brody die like that.

A couple of hours passed as the computer worked and she began to groan as her neck became stiff. Moving her head from side to side, she also rolled her shoulders back. Her chamber filled with a song from her playlist that reminded her of Ilium. A smile formed across her lips as she remembered the sound of his voice and how excited he became every time he learned something new.

Her head bobbed and her eyelids fluttered. This proved much harder to solve than she anticipated, and she finally succumbed to sleep.

But then, she woke up. Only she wasn't quite sure if she was awake or not. Was she dreaming inside of a dream? Was this like that classic movie with Leonardo DiCaprio her grandmother liked to watch? Her eyes flickered open and she noticed a hazy figure in her room. Rubbing her eyes, she strained to recognize who it was standing in the middle of her room.

"Ilium?" she called out.

The figure shook it's head. "You know who I am."

Fear began to grow in her heart as she wondered if the same person who offed Michelle was finally coming for her. However, after staring for a while she uttered with amazement, "You're Dexter!"

The figure nodded.

"But that's impossible. You got sick. You *died*!"

That's what they want you to believe. I did get sick. Terribly sick. But it wasn't from a virus.

Only the last sentence he spoke, his lips didn't move.

This is one weird dream, Avalon thought pinching herself.

That's because you're not dreaming.

Your lips...they aren't moving! And you can read minds? Avalon thought.

I don't have much time. Listen—something happened to me when I went outside. Something strange. I didn't die...I changed. Mutated.

But, Avalon began, *you look the same!*

Yes. Outwardly. But inwardly, he patted his chest, *I can do strange things.*

Like enter rooms undetected? Was it you? Did you leave Michelle in my bed?

Yes. As a warning. He began shaking his head as he stared into space. *He keeps trying it on girls.*

Who is he? And what does he keep trying on girls? Avalon asked.

He thinks you're special. That you can handle it. But I won't let that happen. Cause this isn't stable.

Who is he? What are you talking about?

But Dexter had disappeared just as quickly as he had appeared.

When the wallscreen woke her up the next morning, Avalon was still a bit groggy.

That was some crazy dream!

She turned her head to the side and saw the computer had finished running its latest analysis. The results were grim, with only a 17% efficacy rate for the cure Ilium was working on. Something was missing, but she had no time to think about what could be wrong. She videomessaged her results to Ilium, asking him to work on it when he had spare time.

Why would I dream of Dexter?

She kicked the warm sheets off of her, and hopped out of her bed and down to the floor. The room was flooded with light at the motion. That's when she looked at the floor and noticed the muddy footprints.

Chapter Twelve

Avalon struggled to remain calm. *Is this happening again? Am I going to find another dead body?* Judging by the size of the footprints, it was definitely a man's shoe.

Why would the shoe be covered in mud?

Avalon followed the path of the footsteps. The path went from one wall of her room to the other.

No one can walk on walls! Someone must be playing tricks on me.

Avalon considered calling the guards, but she knew that the prints would probably be long gone by the time they arrived, just like Michelle's body had vanished earlier.

Michelle's body. Avalon sat down on the floor and rubbed her eyes. The dream...had a guy. Dexter. He said he put Michelle's body there on purpose, as a warning, and that he meant her no harm, but someone else did.

Instead of calling the guards, who undoubtedly would not believe her, she did the only thing she knew to do.

She messaged Ilium.

He was there waiting outside of her door in five minutes flat. His cheeks were flushed from running. His hair was still damp, which meant he did not have time to towel dry it. The combination of the dark damp curls around his bright blue eyes gave him an adorable quality which was nothing less than sigh worthy.

Avalon quickly brought Ilium up to speed.

"Since this is the second time this has happened, we can change your room assignment," Ilium suggested.

Avalon shook her head. "No. Dexter doesn't want to kill me, or even harm me. In fact, he may have been trying to help me."

Ilium's face scrunched as he tried to understand Avalon.

"Avalon, you need to rest. You've been pushing yourself too hard," Ilium said.

"No. You must listen to me!"

"Dexter is dead. He is dead. You remember us telling you that right?" Ilium leaned forward to place his hand against her forehead.

Avalon shook her head. "I am not sick. Listen to me, please."

Ilium gave her a look. "Let's assume for a minute that Dexter is alive. Which is preposterous. How would breaking into your room, leaving Michelle's body here, and scaring you half to death *help* you?"

Avalon had to admit he was right. It did sound crazy. "I know," Avalon said with a shrug. "But he said he left her there as a warning. That someone was trying to do something to me."

"Did he say who?"

"No. But it's a male."

Avalon neglected to mention that Dexter spoke to her telepathically. She hoped she really did imagine that part.

With a shrug, Avalon added, "Nothing makes sense right now, I get that. But he also mentioned something about special abilities."

"Special abilities?" Ilium asked.

Avalon nodded.

"You mean, you think it may have something to do with the metahumans Viggo was trying to make?"

Avalon nodded again.

"But here is the thing, Avalon. He was *trying* to make them. We haven't seen one yet."

"But Ilium! You know about the virus and all of the other things they are hiding from us? And how did the body get here and disappear?"

"I don't know. I grant you that. The virus is definitely some kind of eugenics thing probably. But actual metahumans is just…a bit too much."

Avalon sighed.

"But, I don't trust that you're safe alone. Not because of your ideas, but because we don't know exactly what is happening. I am going to walk you to your workstation."

Avalon looked into his piercing eyes and said, "Thank you."

Right before Avalon entered the workstation, Ilium grabbed her hands and held them. *His hands are much larger than I imagined.*

"Listen to me. We are in this thing together. I promised I wouldn't let anyone hurt you," Ilium said.

"Thanks," Avalon said, letting go of his hands and turning to enter the lab.

In the middle of Avalon's daily work queue, the wallscreen lit up and the President told everyone to immediately proceed to the cafeteria for Match Day.

What could be happening now? Avalon thought.

"What is Match Day?" Avalon asked Skylar.

Skylar gave her a look that said *'you should know this already, duh.'* When Avalon still looked confused, Skylar answered, "It's the day we all find out who we'll be mated with."

"You mean it's automated? There's no choice in the matter?"

"Precisely. Both parties fill out questionnaires about their likes, dislikes, etc. This is combined with their DNA data on file and used to provide the best match. The best match, of course, is the match which will result in the healthiest offspring. It is *not* based upon capricious feelings like love which come and go."

Capricious feelings. Love is so much more than that. I understand the government wants to avoid all of the divorces that peaked in the 20th and 21st century, but still. Avalon kept her thoughts to herself and nodded her head. "This is strictly about survival of the species!"

"Exactly. Only about 95% of people match the first round."

"The first round? So there is a second round for the other 5%?"

"Correct. The leftover people that the system, for one reason or another, does not find a suitable mate for are forced to go around asking, begging, fighting, singing, or anything else they can do to find a match that will take them."

Avalon's face twisted.

"Time to go. Don't want to be late," Skylar said.

Avalon couldn't understand how Skylar could just accept everything that they were forced to do in the habitat.

"It's Match Day!" Several girls in the corridor screamed with delight as Avalon rounded the corner to the cafeteria. Skylar did not appear too enthused, and Xin was in his usual nonchalant mode. *Why are these girls excited about a day where instead of mating with the guy of their choice, they are forced to go with whoever an artificial intelligence deems right for them? We have had to sacrifice a lot for the sake of the survival of the species. I am not sure it's something to be cheerful about.*

Skylar did not appear too enthused, and Xin was in his usual nonchalant mode. Ilium bumped into her and whispered, "Should be exciting," sarcastically before he parted to the other side of the room.

Everyone gathered in the middle of the cafeteria, as the table and chairs had been pushed back against the wall. The President stood behind a large podium in the middle of the room, and guards flanked his sides. The Entertainment committee had somehow developed a platform from which the President could speak, and a large wallscreen displayed balloons and celebratory scenes in the background.

"Welcome," the President said.

"Greetings," the crowd answered in unison.

The President smiled as he peered down into the faces of everyone gathered. "You are gathered here today to learn who your mate will be based upon the best genetic pairing which will hopefully result in viable offspring."

Avalon shuddered at the clinical nature with which the President spoke about something so personal.

The President paused to look over the crowd. "Many of you already knew that. However, you're probably wondering why we are having Match Day early."

A hush fell over the crowd.

"Well, we are forced to have Match Day early because the AI has detected that some of you have developed irregularities in your gametes which may affect fertility rates."

Loud gasps erupted throughout the room. There was a slight lilt in the President's voice as he gave his explanation for moving Match Day up.

"Those of you gathered here today are very lucky, as when the others wake up, they will simply be notified of who their partner is. However, the Entertainment chairman deemed a celebratory affair appropriate for you all because you would have been awake the longest by comparison."

The President scanned the room with his eyes. "As you know, whoever the AI selects as your mate will be permanent. Unlike in the world of before, we don't have the luxury of selecting a mate based upon such a quaint idea as love. However, in studying some of the civilizations of the old world, many couples grew to love each other after being in 'arranged marriages', as it was called back then. Each couple will have exactly one year to produce a child. Twenty couples a year will be asked to produce a child on a rotational basis. After any pair has produced two children during their lifetimes, both parties will be sterilized."

Then the President showed a video on a wallscreen where Avalon's father, Dr. Adams, had presented his plan to the President in order to save humanity so long ago. Everyone in the room clapped at the end of the video.

"Let this serve as a constant reminder for why we must make sacrifices for the greater good, not only for today but for the future."

Everyone continued to listen. Avalon held her breath. *Will you hurry up and just call the names?* She glanced up at the countdown clock, hoping the AI would open the doors to the outside even sooner.

Maybe she could run away, and not really participate in this mating program.

"Now, I ask that all of the young men line up against the left wall and all of the girls stand against the right wall," the President ordered.

"Let us begin," The President stated. Behind him, a large screen stood which displayed photos of newly paired couples as their names were called.

As matches were called, the pair was to stand together in the middle of the room and hold hands. The audience was instructed to clap after every pair was named.

"Xin Tu," the President announced.

Xin looked attentively at the President.

"You are matched with Skylar Leatherbury. Congratulations."

Xin accepted the match without a word and walked towards the middle of the room. Skylar stood frozen until the President's eyes fell upon her and she slowly walked towards the middle of the room and grabbed Xin's hand. The audience clapped appropriately.

Skylar's eyes locked on hers. Avalon turned her gaze away. That's when she caught Elena staring daggers towards her. Elena's name had not been called yet. Her group of friends all surrounded her, telling her she was a shoe-in for Kael.

Of course, she is. I am sure if anyone is a match, those two are...

The President continued to call various couple's names, and the audience continued to clap on cue.

"Elena," the President called.

She smirked as all of her friends smiled and winked at her.

Always sure of herself.

"You are matched with Lananias. Congratulations," the President said.

Elena's entire face darkened. Her mouth fell open as others around the room gasped. Avalon turned to look at Kael. However, he closed his eyes and exhaled.

Is he relieved that he doesn't match with Elena?

Lananias was not a bad choice. An Accipio and one of Kael's first cousins, Lananias was considered an excellent candidate. However, he was not Kael.

Elena's feet slowly moved towards Lananias who quickly met her and grabbed her hand. Everyone applauded, but it was definitely not enthusiastic. It was a slow, muted, confused applause.

After that matchup, the sentiment in the room definitely changed from a charged up energy to one more solemn and subdued. People were accepting their matches, but quite a few were not doing so without hesitation. However, no one dared question the AI's choices. More importantly, everyone had the good sense not to challenge the President.

After a while, Avalon noticed her name had still not been called. Before long, no new names were called. Avalon's muscles began to tense as nervousness overtook her. *What's taking so long?* Then the President stopped calling names. Only Kael, Ilium, Avalon, and Raleigh stood against the walls.

"Well, it appears that the computer had difficulty matching these last few. So now the scramble begins for who will sing, fence, or plain, ask for these ladies hands," The President stated.

Murmurs erupted amongst the group. *The President's son, Kael had not been matched? How unusual.* Elena had been matched to another Accipio of her status, but it was not Kael.

Avalon's body threatened to go numb with the realization of being mated forever to either Ilium or Kael. Raleigh's hands were trembling, but she held out her hand to Avalon for support. Avalon grabbed her hand and they stood silently looking at the two boys.

Raleigh's profile flashed briefly across the screen. Avalon took note of the fact that the two of them shared their favorite poem in common: Dylan Thomas's "Do Not Go Gentle Into the Good Night".

"It's going to be OK," Avalon whispered to her.

Inwardly, Avalon did not know who she wanted to be paired with more. Her stomach fluttered for both guys. Ilium was exciting and trustworthy, but Kael was mysterious and an Accipio.

Before Avalon could finish her thoughts, Ilium started to walk towards her. The cafeteria became deathly quiet. Avalon's breath caught. In that same instant, Kael strode towards her as well, except his stride was longer. Ilium stopped walking and Avalon's heart stopped beating as everything unfolded around her in slow motion.

"Avalon, will you be my partner?" Kael asked.

Chapter Thirteen

The entire audience gasped in unison. Avalon's mouth hung open. She glanced back towards Ilium, who stood paralyzed in his spot with his jaw tight. Avalon turned to face Raleigh, who wore a grin and gave her hand a squeeze of reassurance. All eyes were on her. Avalon's lips began to move and she said "Yes." Kael smiled and the crowd erupted with cheer. Avalon's eyes glanced towards the President's unreadable face.

Then Avalon's gaze fell towards Ilium. The only person who did not clap. As the cheers slowed down, the President called for their attention.

"Now, it is time for Ilium to make his choice," the President said. Even though everyone knew only one choice was left.

Ilium stepped towards Raleigh and asked her to be his match. Of course, she answered yes. The audience cheered, but it was much softer and more obligatory than when Kael made his choice.

The President announced with a royal air, "Today is a day of celebration. Thank you for your cooperation and good luck."

Avalon and Ilium were supposed to be happy. *So why did my stomach sink when he held hands with Raleigh?*

Avalon stood, frozen in a moment in time. Kael still stood smiling in front of her, an Accipio. *Isn't this what I wanted? To belong?* An Accipio pairing would make her an Accipio. It would mean she would no longer have to physically work with the others in her computer lab and reduced working hours overall. Instead, she would be a manager, eating synthetic meat behind closed doors, simply reading over reports every so often.

However, something burned within her at the thought of Ilium being with another girl. True enough, she had no reason to dislike her, but she was still upset.

A hand rested on her shoulder. As she turned around, she was face to face with Elena, who was grinning, but not friendly. No, this smile was sinister. Elena's grip tightened around Avalon's shoulder as she shouted, "Congratulations!" to her and then leaned in to embrace her in a hug.

As Elena hugged her, she whispered, "You think you've won by taking Kael, but this has just begun."

When Elena stepped back from the embrace, she once again smiled like they were the best of friends as she walked away with Lananias.

Avalon took two steps towards Elena when Kael grabbed her arm.

Turning her head, she saw him offering a glass.

"Toast?" Kael asked with a smile.

To celebrate the night, a distilled substance made from a certain fungus was served in tall glasses. It bubbled in her glass as it turned different colors— first purple and then red.

Avalon nodded her head and took the glass. They sipped in unison.

Avalon coughed a bit.

"First time?" Kael asked with a wink.

Avalon's cheeks burned as she nodded her head.

"You'll get used to it," he assured her with a smirk.

Avalon caught sight of a few Accipio girls who stole glances her way. Avalon deliberately avoided Elena's gaze.

"Kael…I must ask you something. I know it's not the best time, but Elena seems *very* interested in you. Are you sure you never dated or anything?"

Kael took another sip of his drink as he stared directly ahead.

"Does it matter? I chose you," he said.

Yes, it matters. Just like who Ilium chose tonight mattered. Is Ilium happy with Raleigh? Does he really like her?

Why couldn't the computer find an adequate mate for me? That is probably why the computer had difficulty placing her.

Music began to play, piped through the speakers, and the lights were dimmed. People danced. Kael grabbed Avalon by the waist.

Kael kept in perfect tune to the music. Avalon was also graceful from her many years of classical dance training. Yet, she kept turning her head desperately searching for Ilium.

"Am I boring you?" Kael asked.

"No, not at all," Avalon answered.

"Well, you keep turning your head like you want to dance with someone else."

"I'm sorry, I am sure I am being clumsy."

"No, you're actually quite good," he answered.

And then she caught a glimpse of him in the corner. Both he and Raleigh were sipping on tonic. However, Raleigh's glass was still nearly full, while Ilium had emptied his. *What could that mean? Does that mean he is unhappy? Or could it also mean he is very happy?*

Someone else tapped on her shoulder. Turning around, she was face to face with the President.

"Hello my dear," he said, extending a hand.

She shook it.

The President placed his hand on Kael's shoulder. "I am so glad that my son chose you. Out of everyone here, I always said you had the most potential."

"Why thank you," Avalon said. *Wait, isn't that something a Southern Belle would say?*

"You two carry on. I just wanted you to know that if you ever need anything, you can call on me," he said before walking away.

After a few more rounds of dancing, the speaker came on and said, "That is all for tonight. Lights out in fifteen minutes."

"Aw, man," people said.

"Till next time," Kael said.

Avalon proffered a weak smile and walked away back towards her dorm.

She couldn't stand the thought of Ilium being with another girl anymore. She had to speak to him. So she videomessaged him.

"Hey!" he said, his voice a bit slurry.

"Hey. I need to speak with you."

"OK. I will be over in ten minutes."

Avalon breathed a sigh of relief. Until ten minutes passed. Then fifteen minutes. Which turned into thirty minutes. Frowning, Avalon buzzed his smartwatch. It rung and rung. *Where is he? Why isn't he picking up?*

"Hi, it's Ilium. Leave a message at the beep," his voicemail said.

Frustrated, Avalon decided to just hop into bed and try to sleep. Maybe she could talk to him in the morning.

That's when someone knocked at the door.

Swinging her legs out of her bed capsule, she hopped down and ran to the door. "Ilium!"

"Yep," he said nonchalantly.

"Ilium, did you get my messages? I tried reaching you. Why are you so late?"

"Well…" he said sheepishly, shrugging his shoulders. A red hickey on his neck caught Avalon's attention.

"Ilium!" Avalon shouted angrily.

Ilium perked up. "What?"

"Did you….?" Avalon asked, too afraid to finish the sentence.

"O, No…no we didn't," he answered.

Avalon breathed a sigh of relief. *Wait, why should I care what he does now? He is matched to someone else. And so am I.* "Well listen. I have a theory."

"You and your theories," Ilium said, rolling his eyes.

Avalon squinted at him. "Should we have this talk in the morning?"

Ilium ran his hands through his hair. "Probably. If you want me to remember it."

"Fine," Avalon said, crossing her arms across her chest.

Ilium's smartwatch buzzed and Avalon's attention moved towards it.

"Who is it?" Avalon asked curiosity piqued and with a slight irritation in her voice.

"Raleigh," Ilium said with a coy smile.

Avalon's eyes burned with anger.

"Why won't you admit it?" Ilium asked, tilting his head to the side.

"Admit what?"

With his eyes locked on hers, Ilium moved closer. "That you fancy me. That you were sad tonight with the matches."

Avalon's heart began to pound. They had been matched. She could not defy match orders, so there was no point in admitting anything.

"I will admit no such thing. You and I are strictly frie—"

Ilium's lips locked on to hers, cutting off her sentence. She melted under his embrace, his tender and yet urgent kisses. He grabbed her waist firmly and she gasped under the strength she didn't know he possessed. A dam burst inside of her and she searched for his tongue and desperately kissed back. So many emotions flooded her body as her skin came alive and she tangled her fingers around his dark hair.

In his kiss, she knew all of the feelings he felt for her, and what she felt for him. The kiss spoke louder than words ever could. As he pressed his body tighter against hers, his hands traced up and down her back before they grabbed the bottom of her shirt.

That's when she backed away with slow, reluctant steps.

"What happened? Was I too much?" Ilium asked, his face full of concern.

Avalon shook her head. "It's not that. It's that you have Raleigh now. Remember?"

Ilium nodded his head slowly. "You're right. We shouldn't do this," he said. But his eyes betrayed his emotions.

"But tell me, why can't you just be?" he asked.

"Excuse me?"

"I mean, why can't you just go with the flow like a normal teenager? Just this once."

"You mean act like someone who doesn't have to help save what is left of the human race? Well gee, I wish I could. I wish I could return to a world where the biggest problems in life were grades. But I can't."

"You aren't in this alone," Ilium said, making another step closer.

"Yes, I am," Avalon answered taking one step back.

"No, you aren't," Ilium said, taking two steps closer. Now he was so close she could feel his cool breath across her face.

"But I am. Because I entered this concrete coffin alone and that's how I'll exit it."

"Once again, you're here with five thousand others. You're not alone." He took one hand and placed it around her waist. "Why won't you let anyone get close?"

"Because people die."

Ilium grimaced.

"All right. Have it your way," he said.

Avalon bit the inside of her cheek to prevent herself from rushing right back up to him and resuming their passionate embrace. She wanted Ilium, but she couldn't risk getting attached to him. She had lost so much to the asteroid. Ilium was attached to Raleigh now, whether he liked it or not. Whether she liked it or not.

"It's okay. I am sure it's just the excitement of everything. Rest up, and we'll talk in the morning," Ilium said.

After Ilium left the room, Avalon slid down the back of the door and sat on the floor. Undeniable electricity passed between them, and with his absence the air around her grew colder. His touch made her feel safe and warm. But she didn't want to have half of Ilium, which is all she would ever have since he was matched to Raleigh. Though she wished Ilium had reached her first for Match Day, he didn't. Now she was with Kael, and he was with Raleigh. She might not like it, but she would have to accept it.

This time, sleep came easily to Avalon as she dreamt of Ilium's lips and body pressed up against hers.

Chapter Fourteen

When Avalon woke up the next morning, a hurricane of emotions flooded her body as she remembered Ilium's touch, the way it made her heart race, and his wonderful eyes which were at once sad and yet warm. Involuntarily, she ran the tips of her fingers across her lips as she recalled how wonderful his lips were.

Quickly, she got ready and went to her workstation.

At work and in the corridors, everyone talked about Match Day and who they matched up with. While Xin kept silent on the issue, Skylar did not.

"Well…well." Skylar said. "Should I curtsy or bow to you now?"

Avalon turned towards Skylar and narrowed her eyes. "Look Skylar. I don't want an argument over some silly nonsense like who we are matched with. I am thinking about more important things. I suggest you remember what you told me about Match Day. It is not based on capricious feelings like love and that this is all about the survival of the species. So get back to work. You have already made two mistakes today."

Skylar's mouth hung open before she gradually shut it. A muscle twitched in Skylar's jaw like she wanted to say something back, but she turned away and didn't say anything more on the topic.

"Besides, I'm concerned about Brody right now," Avalon said to the air.

After a moment of silence, Skylar asked into the air, "How is he?"

Doesn't she know already? "Haven't you visited him?"

Skylar grimaced, revealing the answer to be no.

Avalon shook her head. *What is wrong with these people? We work together every day. You would think they would have the decency to check on him. No wonder people are able to go missing and all that happens are a few rumors, and then back to business as usual. I wonder if in our psych evals they also checked for people who had an usually high level of submissiveness and social apathy.*

Avalon looked Skylar in the eyes and said, "He still isn't doing well."

After a hard day at work, Avalon remembered Ilium. *I told him I would videomessage him first thing this morning!* She quickly shot him a message to meet her in the storage room.

"Hey!" Avalon said as he entered the storage room.

"Hi," Ilium said, rubbing the back of his head sheepishly. "I think I embarrassed myself last night."

"No, it's ok."

"Well, still. I apologize."

"It's accepted," Avalon said.

"So, why do you need to talk to me?"

"Well, you know how you said you ran analysis over a lot of people's blood when they woke up?"

"Yeah."

"Did you run an analysis on mine?"

Ilium shook his head. "Now that you mention it, I didn't. Since your pod opened up so unexpectedly, I forgot to. I barely remembered to give you the universal shot."

"Exactly." Avalon took a deep breath and said, "I want you to analyze my blood."

"You? The one deathly afraid of needles?" Ilium chuckled. "Yes." *Hurry up before I change my mind.*

"Well aren't you the brave one! Come over to the infirmary after work and we'll do just that."

Ilium removed a blood sample from Avalon later that day. As he procured it, she gazed into his bright whirlpool eyes which threatened to pull her in with no return. Taking a big breath, Avalon asked, "So, do you really like Raleigh?"

"She's a nice enough girl," he said with a shrug.

"Nice enough. What does that mean?" Avalon asked, trying to sound nonchalant.

"It means she is a nice person. Considering the situation we all found ourselves in. We have always been friends so we share similar interests."

Avalon could sense the word but. So she asked it. "But?"

"But what?"

"It seems you have more to say," she said.

"What do you want me to say?" Ilium asked, turning his gaze back on her. Her stomach did multiple flips. "What about you and Kael? Bet you guys get along really well," Ilium said.

Fishing. "Yeah we get along." *We did get along—but he was no Ilium. I did not get that strange surge of comfort from him.*

"Good," he answered. *This is awkward.*

"What if the AI isn't perfect? What if it makes mistakes?"

Ilium frowned. "Does it matter?"

Avalon stared boldly at Ilium. "Yes. Yes, it does matter."

"How so? How does that relate to us? We weren't matched by the AI. The others were. We were given the ability to choose."

"Ok. We were given the ability to choose. But what about the others? They weren't. And I suspect the AI had help matching people up. Help in the form of a human."

"Like the President?"

"Precisely."

Ilium sighed and folded his arms across his chest. "Even if that were true, there isn't really anything we can do about it."

Avalon took a step closer to him. "There is always something we can do. You know that better than anyone."

"Why would the President match certain people up?" Ilium asked.

"Why does he do anything? Additional control. I am not saying he interfered with everyone's results... Just maybe ours. It's very convenient that we were the ones who the AI couldn't find a match for."

Ilium tilted his head. "You still had a choice, Avalon."

Avalon pouted. "Was it really a choice though Ilium? I mean Kael asked me and he asked me first. He is the President's son."

"Would it have been different if I had asked you first? I was moving towards you."

Avalon grasped his hand in hers. "You know how I feel about you," she whispered.

"Well, I am sorry. I don't think our feelings matter at this point," Ilium said.

Avalon released his hand, and turned to walk away when Ilium said, "Wait."

As she turned around, Ilium added, "What would the President stand to gain by selecting certain people and throwing other candidates out?"

"Maybe some political clout? I mean as a lower class Fulcio matching up with an upper-class Accipio I would imagine it brings some hope to the habitat."

"Something like a Cinderella story you mean?"

"Exactly," Avalon said. "Tell me this before I go. Do you like Raleigh?"

Ilium turned his gaze away and said, "Again, at this point it doesn't matter what either of us feels like. In the end, we are all pawns in the President's game."

An uneasy feeling crept up Avalon's spine. "Yes…but what I am trying to figure out is what game is he playing?"

Chapter Fifteen

Brody's ongoing absence served as a constant reminder of the importance of finding a cure. Xin scolded Avalon on occasion as she began to get some things wrong and fell behind on her work queue. It was increasingly hard to compartmentalize her work life from everything that was happening in her personal life.

Avalon grew to find comfort in meeting Ilium in the storage room. One afternoon they met to discuss the results of her blood test.

"An analysis of your blood revealed some interesting results," Ilium said.

"Like what?"

"Well, as you know, all babies are gestated inside of artificial wombs by government mandate."

"Yeah, that was the law for about twenty years before we entered cryosleep." The government said it was best because mothers with various detrimental addictions could still have healthy babies and receive optimum nutrition levels while having everything monitored. Still confused as to where he was going, Avalon asked, "So what does this have to do with anything?"

"According to my analysis, you lack the promoter region necessary for the virus to bind to, which is why you're immune to the virus."

"Are you saying you think someone interfered with my genetics somehow from when I was in the womb?"

Ilium nodded.

"That is beyond crazy," Avalon said.

"Indeed, but it turned out in your favor," Ilium stated.

"So, perhaps you can somehow use me to save others?"

Ilium nodded. A smile formed on the corners of Avalon's lips.

"So, what do you plan to do with me?" Avalon asked.

"First, I need you to retrieve something from Kael."

"What?"

"I think the missing piece may be hiding in plain sight. I need his smartwatch."

"What do you hope to find on his watch?" Avalon asked.

"It's just a hunch, but I suspect he may have the missing piece for making the vaccine more effective."

Avalon chewed a piece of loose hair. *Kael was many things. A playboy. Confident. Attractive. But was he a killer?*

"Why would Kael have it instead of his father?" Avalon asked.

"Because the President would expect someone to suspect him, but not his son."

Avalon chewed on that tidbit a minute. It was logical. She remembered her father's words, to trust no one.

Avalon locked eyes with Ilium. With a sigh, she asked, "Do you need the watch or just the info on it?"

"Just the info. Once I have it, I think I can change the drug efficiency rate from 17 to 97 percent," Ilium said.

Avalon made several steps towards him.

"You're absolutely brilliant," she beamed as she wrapped her arms around his torso. She could stay there forever, as he was a whole head taller than her, as he patted her hair. She listened in silence as he sniffed her hair. After a couple of moments, they dropped the embrace and Avalon left the room.

A few days later Kael and Avalon had a date in a private dining hall. A Compatio served them a five-course meal. As someone courting an Accipio, Avalon received a red form fitting one-shoulder dress from Kael that was made by a Compatio seamstress. Made of luxurious silk, it hugged her figure in all the right places. Kael also sent a set of earrings and high heel red bottomed shoes to her dorm. The vintage shoes were four inches high and made her calves jiggle a bit. After walking around inside of her dorm to be sure she could walk without falling, Avalon stepped outside where Kael waited for her.

"You look absolutely gorgeous," he said taking her all in.

"Thank you," Avalon said. "You don't look so bad yourself," she added.

Kael wore a dark suit made of the finest material, complete with sterling silver cufflinks, a white shirt, and a navy blue tie. He possessed a swagger and confidence which showed in his posture. Avalon slid her arm inside of Kael's and they strolled together towards the private dining room in Accipio hall.

Kael swiped his hand, and they walked past the Accipio hall doors and stood before large frosted glass double doors. These did not require swiping to enter. Instead, Kael held his eye to a scanner. Once scanned, he held the door open, and Avalon entered the hallway.

The Accipio hall was in stark contrast to the rest of the habitat. First, they were greeted by a gorgeous foyer with a large domed fake skylight, mimicking a gorgeous sunny day. The floor was made of marble tile and the walls were painted a pleasing cream shade with museum quality artwork hanging on its walls. A large fountain stood in the middle of the foyer. Guards surrounded the hallway, protecting the inhabitants therein. Real plants appeared in random alcoves. *The main habitat didn't even have the luxury of artificial plants!*

They continued to walk past the foyer and into the dining room for Accipios. Large crystal chandeliers hung from the ceiling, casting beautiful shadows onto the hardwood floor. Five round tables with white linen tablecloths, crystal goblets, and silverware sat in the room. *How on Earth are they keeping something like this secret?*

Kael pulled her chair out and Avalon sat down. Then he scooted her chair back up to the table and sat down opposite her.

A Compatio waiter immediately flanked her side.

"What would you like to drink?" the waiter asked. He wore a white shirt and a black vest with a black bowtie. His hands were gloved.

"Water, thanks," she said. *Where did they get the material to make these outfits?*

The waiter looked at Kael.

"I will take the same, thanks," Kael said.

Kael smiled at Avalon. She returned his smile and they held hands above the table.

"Did you have a good day today?" Kael asked.

"Yes, thank you. How about you?"

"It was good, thank you," he answered.

"Is that Ilium?" Avalon asked, and as Kael turned his head she quickly touched her smartwatch to his, and downloaded the information. All the smartwatches contained this feature for transferring information, but only an elite few knew about it. Avalon was one of the few since she worked with the computer software team.

When Kael returned his head to face her, he scowled. "That wasn't him."

"Oh. Well, I figured. I mean this place is really fancy and I am sure only the Accipios even know about it."

"Exactly," he answered.

The waiter looked a bit nervous as he walked up to them and asked, "What will you have to eat, Mr. Frost?"

Avalon had paid little attention to the menu, so she looked to Kael to speak first.

"You can call me Kael," Kael said. "And I will take the blackened swordfish with dirty rice,"

Avalon's lips parted open in surprise. Rumors spread about synth-meat but she imagined it could only produce something akin to spam. At most, a hamburger.

"And you madam?" the waiter asked.

"I will have the house salad and rockfish."

"Very good choices," the waiter said before sauntering over to the kitchen. Avalon had never eaten rockfish before, but it sounded interesting.

Avalon and Kael fixed their gaze on each other. Avalon was nervous, which meant a dovetail of questions was going to pop from her mouth. "Have you ever thought about the clouds? About how they stopped forming shapes before the asteroid hit? It was as if they sensed the atmosphere changing," Avalon stated.

"What are you talking about? Do you mean the simulations?"

"No. the real clouds. Before we entered the habitat, they stopped forming shapes. You know how people used to look to the clouds and they could picture the shapes of dogs and cats."

Kael stared into her eyes.

"Why are we having a philosophical conversation when all I want is to get to know you better?" Kael asked.

"You're right," Avalon replied. They sat in silence, with Avalon quietly begging the waiter to return with her food. He was right on time, placing a salad before her made of mixed greens, tomatoes, bleu cheese, and tossed in light vinaigrette. Avalon smiled at the waiter, said 'Thank you,' and then bowed her head to say grace silently.

Once she opened her eyes, Kael looked at her oddly.

"What's wrong?"

"Nothing. It's just... I didn't know people still prayed anymore."

A blush flooded Avalon's face. She quickly stuffed her mouth with the lettuce, trying to stuff the awkwardness by stuffing her stomach.

"That's refreshing," Kael said with a smile on his face.

"What?"

Kael pointed to her plate and said, "You aren't afraid to eat in front of me. Most of the Accipio girls are."

Avalon reflected back to the quartet of otherwise beautiful girls with intentional and large thigh gaps.

"Well, I can't bear the thought of wasting food in our predicament. Food is life."

Kael nodded politely. "You are quite unusual. Very unique."

She reflected on her blood analysis results from earlier. *You don't know how unique.*

After a few moments of small talk, the synthetic swordfish and rockfish arrived. Avalon's eyes widened. It was so much delicious food. It was hard for her to pretend she wasn't angry at the Accipios for herding it for themselves. Trying not to gulp it all down at once, she took a small bite at first.

Kael asked, "Do you like it?"

Avalon took another bite. Did she like it? It had a mild flavor, tender, and a nice flaky texture. It was unlike the bland potato and salad she had grown accustomed to in the cafeteria. "Yes," she said as she dabbed her mouth with a napkin. "Good is an understatement."

Kael smiled. "That's another thing I like about you. You are adventurous."

Avalon took a sip of water. "You like to read, yes? Tell me about your favorite authors?"

Kael listed Ray Bradbury, Suzanne Collins, and George Orwell as some of his favorites.

"What about you?" he asked.

"I like those authors, as well as E.B. White, Mark Twain, and F. Scott Fitzgerald."

After the meal, Kael took her hand and escorted her into a different room.

"Where are you leading me?" she asked.

"You will see. You've got to learn to enjoy surprises," he said with a gleam in his eyes.

Surprises. That's all my life has been lately.

Kael pushed on what appeared at first to be a normal wall, but which opened into a large room. The domed room showed the real midnight sky, full of stars. All around the room were bottles of bubble bath gels, nail polishes, and fresh fruits.

"What is this place?" Avalon asked.

"My sanctuary," he said, taking a step towards her. "I am really glad you're my partner."

Avalon had her skepticism about that with Elena and all. But at the same time, she believed he spoke some truth.

"Why did you do all of this?" Avalon said aloud. Kael was handsome, powerful, and yet he did all of this for her. A Fulcio.

"Why does any male do anything for a female?" he chuckled.

A blush rose to her cheeks.

"You're a rare breed. A sweet girl. Innocent even," he said.

Avalon tried to avert her gaze to the nail polishes. He was so close, she smelled the woodsy scent of his cologne.

Then he swiveled around on his heels and she faced his back.

Have I offended him?

"Thank you, for all of this," Avalon said.

"You're quite welcome." Then he turned around to face her again. "I want to ask you something."

Avalon looked into his face.

"It's about my dad… I feel like there is something wrong with him."

"Well, he is under a lot of stress," Avalon said.

Kael shook his head. "No. It's more than that. He is acting strangely."

"What makes you say that?" Avalon asked.

He paced the floor. "Dad always used to drink caffeinated coffee. Now he only drinks decaf."

"Maybe the doctors detected a heart problem and he had to switch?" Avalon proffered.

"I thought about that too. But then he used to write with his left hand. Now he writes with his right."

"Perhaps he is ambidextrous and never told you?"

Kael nodded. He looked so different in his sanctuary, in this moment. Normally, cool, calm, and confident, he now looked vulnerable.

"This job does strange things to people I am sure. Just being in this habitat does strange things to people," Avalon said, placing her hand on Kael's back.

He turned around and their eyes met. Avalon was suddenly aware of how close they were, of the heat coming off of his body. He was so close she could smell him. He smelled like a cool summer day. Her eyes lowered as she stared at his lips. He leaned down and kissed her, wrapping his strong arms around her waist.

Electricity coursed throughout her body. While it lacked the sweetness of Ilium's kiss, it had an animalistic passion Ilium's lacked.

After a while, Kael escorted her back to her dorm.

Safely inside, Avalon kicked off her high heel shoes. Her feet were throbbing and red with angry marks across the toes.

Kael couldn't be the one they were looking for. He couldn't have the information. Not after tonight. But Ilium was working so hard on every lead, and he would undoubtedly ask about it.

Should I hand it over to him? What if Kael is the bad guy? No, that can't be possible.

Nonetheless, Avalon decided to dial Ilium.

"Yes?" Ilium asked.

"Look, I know it's late at night but I got it."

"Got what?"

"The missing piece. Kael's smartwatch information."

"That is fantastic!" Ilium said.

"But I still don't think it's him." Avalon said.

"You can believe what you want."

"What is it between you two? I mean why don't you like him?" Avalon asked.

"It's a long story."

"Okay. Try me."

Ilium sighed. "I used to be a member of the Accipio class."

"What happened?" Avalon asked.

Ilium gave a long pause before saying, "I falsified my records."

"What do you mean you falsified your records? Did you cheat on a test or something?"

"No. All of my test scores are accurate."

Avalon stared at Ilium's face.

"I, unlike you and the others, was born to normal parents without the aid of a machine."

Avalon gasped.

"That's a good thing! That means you made it all of this way without any genetic manipulation! What's bad about that?"

Ilium's eyes looked appreciative as his lips almost turned into a smile before he looked downcast again.

"Only those born artificially were to enter the habitat to ensure the longest-lived, healthiest humans."

"How did they find out about it?"

"Kael found out about it, but I asked him to keep it quiet. He swore he did, but somehow the President learned of it, and I was demoted."

Avalon shook her head.

"I don't think Kael would do that to you. I think the President did it."

"Sure," Ilium answered. "Avalon…why are you…never mind."

"Why am I what?" Avalon asked.

Ilium struggled to maintain a neutral expression as he looked at Avalon. He couldn't help noticing how beautiful she looked in a dress. The truth was, he couldn't help thinking about her at all. An ache rose in his chest as he asked, "Why are you so dressed up?"

"That's how I got the information, by having dinner with Kael."

Ilium visibly bristled. He was thankful he wasn't standing in the room with her. Being so close to her in person without being able to kiss her was becoming too much to bear. He struggled to think of something more to say.

"Please don't do that," Avalon said.

"Do what?"

Avalon let out a huff in exasperation. "Look, I sent you the smartwatch info. Let me know when you receive it," Avalon said.

"Got it," Ilium answered when he received it on his smartwatch.

Avalon signed out of the videomessage.

The next morning, Ilium walked into the infirmary. Brody trembled and sweat with dangerously high temperature. Ilium recognized these as signs of the final stage.

Ilium quickly went to work at looking at the information in Kael's smartwatch.

I don't know what Avalon sees in Kael. I mean yeah he is the President's son and all, but he is not a good guy. Avalon deserves better.

After more than an hour, he still didn't see anything. Most of the information consisted of emails, communications, and game scores.

Why does she have to be matched to Kael? He doesn't deserve her. The way her whole face lights up like a sparkler when she greets you.

After another two hours passed, Ilium scrubbed his eyes as his vision blurred.

Perhaps, Avalon is right. Maybe Kael doesn't have anything to do with this.

Then he decided to double click on one of his game scores.

Hm…That's odd. This score is written weirdly. Like a hexadecimal code.

Ilium went to work sketching out the code.

This is no accident. This must have something to do with the virus.

After matching a compound to the code, Ilium came upon a formula which he ran through computer simulations.

"99% efficacy rate," the AI said.

Ilium smiled.

Well, I'll be. Kael had the missing link all along. But he isn't smart enough to come up with this by himself. Not at all. He had to have help.

Sweat beaded on his forehead as he went to work prepping the ingredients to be delivered intravenously. He constantly looked over his shoulder at Brody whose breaths were getting raspier.

Ilium carefully reached into his drawer for a syringe. Brody's once strong broad back now shrunk around him. His sweat soaked hair stuck to his forehead. An unruly five o'clock shadow formed around his once smooth face and grew down his nape.

With sweat forming on his brow, Ilium filled the syringe. According to his simulations, the medicine should take effect over the course of the next four hours.

Ilium walked over to Brody and grabbed the IV line to his wrist. With a deep breath, he began to administer the drug when two broad chested guardsmen with electric batons entered the room.

"Hello, how may I help you?" Ilium asked, stopping half way with the administration.

"You are under arrest," the tallest guardsman answered.

"Under arrest! What on earth am I under arrest for?" Ilium asked as the tallest guardsman placed cold metallic handcuffs around his wrists.

"You are under arrest for hacking into a computer system and for trespassing," the short guardsman answered.

"That is two strikes!" Ilium yelled.

The taller guardsman nodded his head.

"But once you have three strikes, you are automatically kicked out of the habitat!"

They ignored his decries and continued on with their recitations. "You will be judged and sentenced for these crimes by the President."

"But who will run the clinic?" Ilium asked.

"Kael has medical training as an assistant and will fill in for you during this time."

"Kael!" Ilium's blood boiled at the name. "Well, at least let me finish administering this medicine to my patient!"

"Kael can handle that," one of the guards said.

Just as the guardsman said his name, Kael emerged from behind them. Ilium's eyes narrowed as he put the pieces of the puzzle together, too little too late.

The guards escorted Ilium out of the room and down the corridor to the holding cell. The holding cell was located in Accipio Hall, and no one had actually seen it in person besides the President.

Chapter Sixteen

On her lunch break, Avalon searched for Ilium. After five minutes passed, she stood in line without him. After grabbing her standard lunch, she sat down by Skylar. *Where is he? Is he with Raleigh?*

"So, you're going to rejoin the group today, huh?" Skylar remarked.

"I never left," Avalon said.

"Sure, sure. Where is lover boy?" Skylar taunted.

"If you mean Kael, I don't know. If you mean Ilium, I also don't know and I was going to ask if you had seen him?"

Skylar rolled her eyes. "No."

It's unlike Ilium to skip lunch. It's unlike anyone to skip lunch except for those skinny Accipio girls. Avalon pressed a button on her smartwatch and private messaged Ilium. "Where are you?"

After the thirty-minute lunch ended, she still had no answer from Ilium. Now she began to worry as her heart raced and her stomach tossed and turned in tune to the thoughts coursing through her mind.

"Are you ok?" Xin asked. Sweat beads formed across her brows.

"Sure," Avalon answered and wiped her forehead. Ilium would have been able to detect the slight lilt in her voice. Thankfully, Xin did not.

The rest of the workday was exceedingly difficult to finish. Avalon kept staring at the military time clock, which ran backwards. Finally, the work day ended. Ilium was not going to ignore her anymore. She logged off from her workstation and marched straight into the infirmary to check on Ilium and Brody. After Avalon swiped her wrist over the door sensor, she was shocked to find Kael standing where Ilium should have been and wearing Ilium's stethoscope around his neck.

"Hi, Kael," Avalon said steely.

"Hello," he answered.

"Where is Ilium?"

"I hate to be the one to tell you this, my love, but Ilium was arrested."

Avalon stood in her spot a moment before laughing loudly.

"Arrested? For what?"

"For being a traitor," Kael calmly answered, moving closer to Avalon with open arms.

Avalon-backed away.

"A traitor? There can be no such thing. We have no real form of government. Besides you and I *both* know that Ilium is harmless."

"But, we *do* have a form of government, my dear. Remember, my father is the President? And I am his son. We have guards to police."

"You mean to protect?"

"To police and to protect. The fact remains that while you may think Ilium is harmless, he is alleged to have committed two crimes which resulted in two strikes. We must maintain order in this environment. We can't be like we were before, with all of that chaos and mayhem." Kael studied her face before continuing, "I trust that you were unaware of these alleged crimes?"

Ignoring his insinuation, she asked, "What crimes did he allegedly commit?"

"He broke into the computer systems and he trespassed into the science lab. These are serious offenses. As you know, trust is a very important concept with us confined to a small space like this. We must all follow order and rules."

Avalon rolled her eyes at his political diatribe. "Where is he being held?"

"The holding cell."

"What are they going to do to him?" Avalon asked, the pitch of her voice rising as her muscles tensed.

"I don't know what his final sentence will be. For now, they will just keep him in the holding cell. But you can only visit him once a week. His cell is located in the Accipio hall."

Avalon stared at Kael. "How can you stand here and do this? Pretend to take over Ilium's position?"

"I am only following orders. I told you that. Ilium has broken the rules—"

"I *heard* you the first time. I also didn't believe you the first time," Avalon said brusquely.

"Wait!" he yelled but she had already left the room. Before she left the room, she viewed Brody's monitor from the corner of her eye. All of his vital signs were declining. *What the heck is happening! I thought the cure was supposed to work!*

That night Avalon watched the clock tick as she tossed and turned. Her thoughts also tossed from Brody to Ilium. *We worked on that cure for so long. The computer said it was 99% effective. Is Brody in that unlucky 1%? Surely not. But then again...But we can't lose Brody! Something isn't right... And poor Ilium...Is he afraid? Is he hurt? What is he thinking? How did the President discover that Ilium broke in, but not me...* no matter how many times she ran everything over in her head, something didn't add up.

Ilium was one of her biggest sources of hope in this dismal habitat where everything was a false simulation of the real life that they would never see again. His warm and authentic personality illuminated not only the habitat but her life in it. No, he could not be left alone to endure his fate.

What would his fate be? What were these people capable of? They were already conducting illegal experiments on Compatios...are they going to experiment on Ilium?

As the wheels in her mind turned and thoughts formed and split off like rivers, an alert she placed on Brody's monitor went off.

His oxygen sat is declining rapidly!

Immediately, she dialed Kael. "What's going wrong?" Did you do anything?"

"No. I have this under control. Wait- how did you know something was wrong?"

Avalon jumped out of her bed capsule and ran to the infirmary. Brody's face was very blue. The cure must not be working. "Brody! Brody! Hold on okay?" Avalon said as she held his hand. He appeared nonresponsive. Kael appeared nervous.

"We need Ilium!" she yelled.

"A real doctor!"

"I am just as good as him!" Kael calling yelled back. "I am not calling for him."

Frantic, Avalon searched the room. Several bottles of various sizes and colors were strewn on the counter but she couldn't identify anything.

Then, on the floor, next to Kael's shoe, was a half empty syringe.

Avalon picked it up.

"What are you doing? Throw that away. You should be wearing gloves," Kael admonished.

Avalon rolled her eyes and plunged the contents into Brody's IV.

"You don't know what was in that thing! You could be killing him! I should have you—"

"Arrested? Like Ilium?" Avalon interrupted. "Be my guest, because if you think I am going to let Brody die due to your ignorance, you are very mistaken."

Kael stood there in silence with his mouth slightly ajar. Clearly, no one had spoken to him in that manner before.

A loud and long beep sounded as the monitor showed a flat line.

"No!" Avalon yelled as she beat on his chest. Tears rolled down her face.

"No! No! No!" she repeated and reached for a defibrillator.

"You don't know how to use that!"

"I don't have to! The AI does it after I hit start. Get out of my way!" she yelled.

Avalon placed the pads on his chest and hit start. The first shock was administered. Avalon held her breath. The flat line was still there, and his chest did not rise and fall.

Avalon dialed up a higher shock and when the wave of electricity hit his body, she waited longer to see if it would work.

"He's gone," Kael whispered coming up from behind.

Avalon shook her head from left to right.

"He can't be."

Kael tried to touch Avalon's shoulder.

"Don't!" she gleamed, picking up a scalpel and holding it in her hand.

"There's no need to get violent," Kael said stepping away.

"Just leave. Just leave because you're of no help here."

Kael left the room and Avalon rested her head on Brody's shoulder.

She looked at the time on the clock, so she would know his time of death.

Brody, who was once so strong and vibrant, was no more. Avalon raised her head from his shoulder and looked into his eyes. She closed his eyes, which bore no more light.

For several hours, Avalon remained in the room, unable to fully process everything. She didn't feel right leaving his body without anyone to properly dispose of it. In the old world, he would have had a proper burial and funeral. Friends and family would have mourned his death. In this habitat, people died and things happened but because it didn't affect the people who mattered nobody cared. It just wasn't on the radar.

What lie would the President come up with next? How would they explain away Brody's death?

Despite the fact she had not known him but for a few days, he had already become a friend.

Suddenly, the room doors opened and the Council entered the room. They moved almost as one unit, like the videos she used to watch as a child of soldiers marching together.

Their almost albino appearance was quite arresting, their almost noiseless entry even more so. Avalon startled.

"We have come to take the body," they announced without even bothering to look at her. It was as though they were talking to the air. As though they couldn't see her, or just simply wouldn't directly acknowledge her.

Avalon wanted to ask a million questions. Where were they taking his body? What were they going to do with him? What lie would they create to explain him away? But to anger the Council meant courting death. And she didn't want to do that. With Ilium locked up, someone had to tell the story.

Avalon stepped aside as they came and lifted his body unto a stretcher and zipped it close inside of a black body bag.

That's when it truly hit her. That would be the last time she would ever see him alive.

Her knees buckled, but this time, no one was there to catch her.

She fell to the ground. It was too much going on. Too much to handle without Ilium. After lying on the ground for an hour, way after the Council left, Avalon sat up.

If this was a game of chess, Avalon no longer wanted to be a pawn. It was time to make moves across the board.

Avalon was sick and tired of life happening to her. She made a promise to herself that from that day forward, she would change that.

Chapter Seventeen

Ilium's holding cell was a hollow cube of bullet and shatterproof glass which offered no privacy. One commode and steel sink were in the far left corner. The overhead fluorescent light flickered and buzzed while the lone lumpy mattress in the right corner was pitifully undersized. Noticeably absent was a wallscreen. Except for the red digital clock hung in the middle of his cell, there would be no way for Ilium to tell day from night, night from day.

Ilium spent the first day pacing the floor of the holding cell and doing sit ups and pushups to keep busy. His mind kept thinking about Brody and if the medicine was enough.

That night, as Ilium lay on the lumpy mattress, he thought about how he became a member of the habitat. The odds were against him winning entry into HOPE, but he won, beating out over 1000 others who took the test for physician. After that, he underwent countless psychological and physical exams. He tried to think of this holding cell as being similar to the simulation where he was isolated for 72 hours to test for any cracks in his psyche.

By the second day, Ilium asked for a book to read. He received a nonfiction biography of the President.

Although it was the only company he had, it was hard to concentrate on the dry, boring biography of the President. He pressed a button on the tablet and a 3-D holographic news clip appeared from the President's last days outside before entering the habitat.

A pretty young blonde girl in a red dress was speaking outside of the habitat area as it was entering its last stage of construction. The sun-kissed newscaster was reporting on the protestors, as well as the fact that the world was set to end in three weeks. Protestors marched behind her. The protestors mainly consisted of people who were not selected from the lottery and those who failed the selection and aptitude tests. They were allowed to peacefully protest about 500 feet from the site. Some of the protestors carried signs which talked about how the project was a waste of taxpayer money, how everyone should die together, or how it was unfair to save a select few.

Barbed wire fence, electric fencing, a large stone wall, numerous lights, and cameras, along with security guards watched over the habitat as it was being built. A large white sign was posted outside which read in large red letters, RESTRICTED AREA. NO TRESPASSING BEYOND THIS POINT. A second sign read WARNING MILITARY INSTALLATION. The words in fine print at the bottom of the sign were the scariest: Use of deadly force authorized. The sign creators did not even bother to bold or otherwise highlight the most important part of the sign. Construction crews were only allowed to work on one section of the habitat at a time before they were laid off.

After the newscaster finished speaking, Ilium turned off the news clip. *What other rooms could be hidden here?*

Just as Avalon headed down the corridor to see Ilium as most of the rest of the habitat slept, Raleigh grabbed her hand.

"Are you going to visit Ilium?" she asked.

"Yes," Avalon said with a hint of irritation.

"He likes you more," Raleigh said, lowering her gaze to her nail-bitten hands.

"Don't say that," Avalon said as she touched Raleigh on the shoulder. "Ilium continues to love you more each day. He is truly devoted to his duty and doing what it takes to survive."

"That's just it—it shouldn't *be* a duty. That word smacks of a chore. A responsibility."

"He *is* a responsible person."

Raleigh nodded her head in agreement.

"I remembered who you remind me of by the way. Who you resemble."

"Really?"

"Ilium keeps a photo of his parents with him in his pocket. Its super crumpled up, but laminated. His mother was very beautiful, very classy, and the spitting image of you."

That explains some of the immediate friendship we felt towards each other.

"Oh, and I'm so sorry about Brody," she added.

The President had concocted a lie which quickly spread about Brody's death. Something about he had a peanut butter allergy and somehow came into contact with a strong dose.

"It was really tragic," Raleigh said.

Avalon just stared at her. *You don't know anything.*

"Thank you. I truly appreciate that," Avalon answered. As Raleigh turned around, Avalon noticed her

neck had a red spot.

"Raleigh," Avalon said as she pointed to the girl's neck. Raleigh's eyes grew wide and her cheeks reddened at Avalon's remark.

"You haven't. Ilium has only been in the holding cell three days. Plus, you know it's against the law."

"I know! But did anyone think that maybe all of us were falling in love with other people before this whole Match Day mess? There is a reason some of us were impossible to match, even for the AI."

Avalon contemplated what Raleigh spoke. How much it mirrored her own sentiments. So there were some people who weren't completely emotionless or narcissistic.

"Are you going to?"

"No. I won't tell. But if you ever, and I mean *ever*, break Ilium's heart in any way, I promise to do something far worse," Avalon threatened.

Avalon walked away from Raleigh and towards the holding cell.

"Breaking out is a third strike," Ilium said as Avalon spoke to him. Avalon visited him the third day after finding out that he was arrested. Ilium was so relieved to see Avalon that a smile formed across his face for the first time in three days. His skin looked desiccated, and his eyes were bloodshot from lack of slumber.

"I really need you to focus on staying alive right now and to stop focusing on following the rules," Avalon whispered.

"So are you admitting you like me?" Ilium asked, his voice pregnant with hope.

Avalon rolled her eyes and then cracked a smile.

"What took you so long to visit?"

Avalon ignored his first question but answered the second. "If I came to visit you on the first two days of the week, the guards would have been more vigilant. By letting a few days pass, and thus some of their adrenaline drop, I anticipate they won't be so vigilant. There's only thirty minutes left for visitation and most everyone is asleep. Look behind me, the guards themselves are stretching and yawning right now."

"I can't let you break me out. It would mean a strike for you too, and I can't risk that. I am not worth getting a strike for," Ilium said.

"Well, if you think I am going to sit on the outside and act like life is just dandy without you in it, you're sadly mistaken. Leaving you here is not an option."

Ilium's eyes met Avalon's for a moment.

"So what do you plan to do?" Ilium asked with a sigh, realizing he would lose an argument with Avalon.

"The less you know, the better," she answered. "Just follow my lead."

A Guardsman entered the room. "Your time is up," he said.

Avalon nodded her head and waved to Ilium. In one swift move, she managed to spin around on her heels and quickly grab the guardsman's electric baton from his belt and use it on him. A second, shorter guard entered the room. She hid in a recess in the wall and took care of him too with the baton as he stooped down to look at his partner. Noting a tranquilizer gun on the second guard, Avalon snapped it up.

"Where did you learn krav maga?" Ilium asked.

"My Dad wanted me to know a few things before I entered the habitat. He knew I might be singled out and he wanted me to be able to stand firm."

"Well, you could certainly teach me a few things," Ilium said.

Avalon smirked as she grabbed the guardsman's wrist and waved it in front of Ilium's cell. As the door opened, Avalon said, "Take this tranquilizer gun and if you see someone chasing us, use it!"

Avalon and Ilium navigated the corridor. Most of the others were returning from the cafeteria, so Avalon blended in and Ilium kept close behind her. Avalon kept looking over her shoulder, checking to ensure no one followed them. Each time she looked, she didn't see anyone. Avalon and Ilium quickly ducked into the storage room. Now that they were alone, Avalon allowed the wave of pure adrenaline to hit her, letting a smile creep on her face.

"We did it. You're out!" she said, throwing him some brown scrubs to put on instead of the orange scrubs he wore while in the holding cell. He turned his back as he changed into them.

"Yeah, but we aren't home free. I am sure every guardsman is on the lookout for us," Ilium said. The storage room was kept cooler than the rest of the habitat, so his breath came out as little puffs of clouds.

Avalon twisted her neck from side to side, to let off some of the kinks which had formed due to stress.

"Here, let me help you with that," Ilium offered as he placed his hands on her shoulder. Her eyes closed as the gentle pressure of his hands melted her stress away.

"Goodness. Stressed much?" Ilium said.

"Yes," her eyes dimmed as she thought of Brody. "Something didn't work Ilium. With the cure."

Ilium dropped his hands from her shoulder and turned around to face her.

"What do you mean, something didn't work?"

Avalon exhaled. "He is gone."

Ilium didn't respond for a few moments, resting his head up against a wall as he closed his eyes.

"But the computer said—" he began.

"I know," Avalon cut him off. "The only thing I can think of is that maybe he is in the minority."

Ilium shook his head. "I don't believe so. I just don't believe those odds."

Avalon nodded in agreement.

"You know that means…"

Tears formed in the corner of Avalon's eyes. "I know."

Ilium wrapped his arms around her and held her close.

"It's going to be alright," he whispered. "I will figure something out."

"But it's too late. Too late for Brody," Avalon stammered.

"Maybe. But we can still save the others," he said.

Ilium's perpetual state of hope inspired and perplexed Avalon. She supposed that was in part, what made him such a great physician.

After they sat together a spell, Ilium said, "As much as I would love nothing more than just to live here forever with you, there's no food here. And my stomach is growling."

That caused a small smile to form on Avalon's face.

"You're right," she said, rising to her legs.

She stuck her ear to the door and counted to five minutes. "I think the hall is pretty silent now. Let's duck back out there," Avalon said.

She swiped her hand over the door and immediately something hard hit her in the head before she collapsed to the hard cement floor.

Chapter Eighteen

Avalon opened her eyes briefly only to shut them again because it was so bright. Once she reopened them, she spotted microscopes and other lab equipment on countertops. Several wallscreens were monitoring some experiments and displaying real-time results in a continuous stream. Some rats, which somehow managed to survive the effects of the asteroid, were behind glass hooded cages. Various shapes and sized bottles and containers littered the room. *Viggo's lab.* Avalon tried to sit up, but could not. Her hands and feet were tied to the chair. Ilium was also tied to a chair. He appeared unconscious, with a four-inch long gash across his forehead. *That's going to need stitches.* Her shirt had a few specks of red as well. *Is that from Ilium or me?* Panic welled up inside her. She tried to force it down and focus the adrenaline coursing through her veins on assessing her new situation. The President's chief scientist, Viggo, closed the distance between them and stood two feet in front of her face.

"I see that you've decided to join the party, Miss Adams," the bespectacled thirty-five-year old said.

As her head still spun, making the walls appear to be melting in front of her, she paused to take a deep breath and clear her head. After a moment, she managed to ask, "What...... have...... you...... done?"

Viggo analyzed her a moment before answering, "O, just a little pistol-whipping to the head. You will recover. From *that* at least," Viggo said as he parceled out his words with great care.

As Avalon tugged at the ties around her hands and feet, she asked, "Why am I here?"

Viggo smiled slightly and said, "Playing the innocent I see. You see, I already know that you and your little friend, Ilium, have been snooping around my files."

"You must be mistaken," Avalon answered, her eyes never leaving his.

"Don't try me, Avalon. We both know that you all were snooping around."

Avalon said nothing but stared at her captor with eyes that could bore a hole through steel.

"What are you planning to do with us? Torture is not allowed. It's against the convention—" Avalon stated before being cut off by Viggo.

"Who said anything about torture, my dear girl? We have progressed far from those barbaric times. Goodness no. You will tell me anything I want *willingly* in due time," he said. Avalon shuddered but tried not to let him see it.

"Viggo. You were my father's friend. His confidant. You know me. This isn't like you."

"Oh, yes," Viggo said. "Your father. Dr. Adams. World-renown scientist. Savior of humanity. But this conversation isn't about him. It's about you."

The jealousy present in his voice was not lost on Avalon. She thought Viggo was a friend of her father's. But it was clear he was merely gunning for an opportunity to shine. To ride her father's coattails.

From his white lab coat pocket, Viggo produced a tablet and placed it in front of her. She immediately recognized her formula for a cure to the scourge on its 3-D holographic surface. He spun the formula around with his hands.

"I don't want to harm you. Unless I have to. But this is why you are here," he said, pointing to the formula.

His reassurances meant nothing to her. Every word he had said to her about being concerned for her safety was a lie.

"Where did you find that?" Avalon hissed, the terror she once had fading into anger.

"Where do you think I found it?" he smiled showing teeth. His smile turned Avalon's stomach.

"The thing is I didn't find it at all. I made it."

Avalon tried to hide her shock. *It made sense that if he made the virus, he would also have the cure.*

Viggo continued. "The question you should be asking is, why did I let you have it?"

Avalon knew she wouldn't like his answer. Avalon's wrists rubbed raw as she attempted to escape from the restraints. She looked around the room for any way to escape.

"I let you have it because the "cure" you stole from Kael's smartwatch was fabricated."

"You're wrong. It is 99% effective. You're just trying to scare me," Avalon spat.

"Yes, that is what the computer said isn't it. But that's what I told the computer to say."

Avalon could not believe her ears. All this time, she and Ilium thought they were doing good and helping to save people. Viggo knew the whole time. Not only did he know, but he played along with them. All the while probably sitting back laughing.

"Why?" Avalon's voice broke. She thought about Brody and how he had already contracted the illness and died. "Why are you doing any of this? Pretending to help people when you are actually killing them?"

"First, I owe you no explanation. But, since, I have a captive audience, I guess I will divulge." He paused before continuing, "At first, I had no intentions of killing my subjects. I *wanted* them to live. That was the goal of my overall research. But…as always…anomalies crept up in the data. The people…I mean *subjects*…did not always react or behave as predicted. I figured I had to obtain subjects where they would be least noticed as missing."

Avalon's mind struggled to keep up with the information. Yet, she decided to keep peppering him with questions, desperately trying to delay the inevitable.

"So, that is why you chose the Compatios. They were the easiest targets?"

"Aren't you the smart one," he said rolling his eyes. She couldn't help but notice how dark and rodent-like they were behind his glasses. It was true what her father said. She could trust no one.

"Is the President in on this too?" Avalon asked.

At this, Viggo laughed.

"That idiot would *never* go along with my plans. He is too principled. He would rather we all die together than some of us survive and live."

This bit of news blindsided Avalon. She always presumed that the President was the one ultimately behind everything. If the President wasn't behind this, then someone close to him must have been.

"Well, if not the President, who?"

"Those smarter than the President. Those able to help him choose the best path."

"You mean to lie to him?"

"Yes. If you must use such terminology. It is the only way he would go through with what he is about to do."

What he is about to do. What is he about to do? Avalon thought but decided to ask another question. "What about the Council?"

"You sure have a lot of questions," Viggo said. "The Council are all part of my first successful attempt at radiation proof humans."

"But they all look so similar," Avalon said.

"Well, if by similar you mean they all have no body hair that was one of the side effects of the experiment." Then his nose crinkled. "Unfortunately, I was unable to secure a female who could survive the process."

Avalon wanted to call him all kinds of names, but at the same time, she wanted to extract the most information she possibly could from him. Although, if she died, she didn't know how it would be of much help.

"What is Code BK Max? If you're going to kill us, we at least need to know what we are dying for." Avalon asked.

"Now we are headed in the right direction, asking the right questions," Viggo said with a sickeningly arrogant smile. "Code BK Max refers to going outside. A few months ago, I asked a brave young man to venture outside on a recon mission."

He must be talking about Dexter.

"What happened?"

"Something terrible happened to him. He was not supposed to be allowed to return to the habitat because he had been exposed to too much radiation. However, the AI somehow malfunctioned and allowed him to enter."

Avalon continued to struggle in vain with the restraints. She wished someone knew where they were and would come to save them. But no one would think to look for them in Viggo's lab. Why should they?

Avalon decided to ask another question. "Well, where is he now? Is he Ok?"

"I appreciate how you are trying desperately to bide your time by asking all of these questions. It would work too if my plans weren't absolutely perfect."

Avalon gritted her teeth.

Viggo continued. "I will indulge since all we have is time. We shut off all the rooms except one where we quarantined him. After just six hours, he was declared dead from radiation poisoning."

Avalon knew it was a stupid question but she asked it anyway. "Are you certain he was dead?"

Viggo laughed. "Yes. He was dead. Why do you ask?"

Avalon remembered the muddy footprints in her room and Michelle's body.

Avalon ignored his question as she remembered what Dexter said to her in her 'dream' that night.

Viggo chuckled. "Go ahead and ask me. I see a question written all over your face and lips."

Avalon didn't want to placate Viggo anymore, but she did have one major question left. "What exactly do you plan to do with me?"

"As I said before, I do not *wish* to harm you."

Confusion rose in Avalon as blood rushed and congealed in her veins, but she recognized her limitations while in restraints.

"You are very special," Viggo said. "The funny thing is you don't even know it. You were told that your pod was opened by accident. A result of an electrical error. But that is what I *wanted* you to believe."

Avalon's eyes widened.

"Yes, my dear. It was I. I opened your pod early because the AI assured me that a female in this habitat was already immune to high levels of radiation. That she was the missing piece."

"Why would you do such a thing? I could have died!" Avalon spat.

"You could have died, but you didn't, because I knew Ilium was there and would discover you in time. I also knew all about his little blood sampling project. Unfortunately, he did not sample your blood immediately upon waking." Viggo said rolling his eyes. "I guess he was too struck by your beauty."

"Then how do you know for certain that I am immune to radiation if you didn't obtain a blood sample?" Avalon asked.

"Because I pumped your room with increasing levels of radioactive air at night. Shut off the other air vents to direct it to just your room. You showed absolutely no deleterious effects. It was absolutely remarkable."

"It was absolutely crazy!" Avalon screamed. "And *you* have gone crazy!"

"No need to make all that fuss. Unless you want to wake your little boyfriend." Viggo answered.

Avalon scrutinized the room behind Viggo's face. On a long metallic table sat three plastic tubes full of blood. She didn't fully notice the bandage on her upper arm until he mentioned sample. Her head still reeled from being hit over the head with a pistol.

"You have no right...None at all," Avalon hissed as she began to feel woozy again. *You are supposed to eat something after donating that much blood.*

"That may be true. But equally true is the fact that you are what I've been searching for since I entered this place. You will be the wellspring from which humanity will survive."

Avalon's eyes widened.

"What do you mean?" Avalon asked hesitantly, trying to conceal the nervousness racing through her body.

"You know what I mean my dear," Viggo said as one-half of his lips curled up. Avalon shuddered at the sight. Viggo laid one of his cold, clammy hands on top of her upper arm.

Her gaze fixed on Ilium. *How on earth am I going to get us out of this mess?*

Chapter Nineteen

Viggo walked away from Avalon for a moment and grabbed a water bottle from a table beside him. After taking a sip of water, he continued, "Do you know why everyone isn't currently awake in this habitat?"

"I am tired of playing these stupid games with you. If you're going to kill me or whatever, go ahead and do it," Avalon said.

"My dear. You have the wrong idea. I have no intentions of *killing* you."

Again, Avalon's mind raced and she did not like where her thoughts were headed. He had mentioned several times that he did not want to harm her, but he would anyways. Yet, now he said he did not plan to kill her. So what was he planning to do?

"Because the President wanted to only wake up a certain amount of people at a time. That way, he could maintain order," Avalon answered.

Viggo smirked. "That is what he was told. But it doesn't mean it's the truth."

Avalon licked her lips. "What do you mean?"

"Five thousand people are in this habitat," he said stating the obvious. "But not all of them deserve to live."

"What do you mean?"

"Exactly what I said. Only the strongest and fittest deserve to live and survive. Those who come from backgrounds which historically have been deemed undesirable…well…"

"You wouldn't!" Avalon shouted.

His words slammed into her like a freight train. Her head throbbed. *The cryofluid. This freak in front of me was one of the people tasked with ensuring we were put to sleep properly. The silvery fluid we all swam in which was meant to sustain life…*

"I would and I did. The others will never awake," Viggo finished.

Avalon's whole body went numb.

"You sick—" Avalon began.

"Oh my dear, that is just the half of it. I think you will enjoy seeing the completion of my brilliant plans," Viggo said.

This has to be some kind of nightmare from which I will awake soon, she prayed.

A wallscreen lit up beside them. Immediately, clips of a video played of Ilium administering the inoculation shots to everyone as soon as they woke up. At the end of the clip, the President appeared sitting behind his large desk. "My friends, I hate to interrupt your important tasks to relay some troubling news. The very man you entrusted your very lives with, Ilium, has been quietly poisoning select individuals."

People in their workstations across the habitat gasped.

"That is right," the President continued. He is the direct cause of at least five lives which have been lost in this habitat. The exact number is still in question."

The President paused for effect as the blood drained from the faces of his people. Others screamed as others cried.

Ilium shook his head from side to side, as consciousness finally returned to him. Avalon tightened her grip on her chair, trying with all her might to break free, to no avail.

"Trying to leave before the show ends, I see?" Viggo said.

Avalon leaned forward, baring her teeth like an animal about to attack.

"Such beautiful teeth. It would be a shame to lose them," Viggo threatened.

Avalon sat back in her chair. Ilium continued to wake up and finally asked, "Where are we?"

"Welcome to the party *mi amigo*," Viggo said.

"What…what am I doing here?" Ilium asked. His head swirled as he tried to orient himself to the situation. Avalon was tied up to a chair, and when he struggled to move his arms, he realized his arms were tied down as well. His chest tightened with fear.

"You're being held here for killing five inhabitants via your inoculation shots," Viggo calmly stated.

"What? I did no such thing!" Ilium shouted, trying to break free of his arm ties.

"Are you trying to leave too? You two are so rude. No wonder you make the perfect couple."

"Shut up!" Avalon yelled.

The President continued talking on the wallscreen. "This is not Ilium's first strike. Along with the other two strikes he has incurred, this means that Ilium has three strikes."

A loud cheer erupted throughout the habitat.

"The Council and I met in an emergency meeting to discuss the urgency and hideousness of these strikes. It was determined, via unanimous vote, that Ilium will not be tried by his peers, but instead, would be tried by the Council. He was found guilty by the Council."

People continued to gasp as the President surveyed the crowds gathered around the multitude of wallscreens.

"By virtue of the power vested in me, I pronounce sentence of expulsion from the habitat for Ilium," the President continued.

The wallscreen broadcast ended, and roars continued to erupt throughout the habitat. Inhabitants screamed about Ilium, calling him a traitor, a murderer, and a liar.

That's when it hit Avalon. Viggo wasn't going to hurt her physically. Of course not. He needed her. He was going to hurt her by hurting Ilium.

"You can't do this!" Avalon and Ilium yelled at Viggo.

"I can, and I have," he answered smugly.

A Guardsman entered the room, one of those that Avalon had knocked out with the baton earlier. He untied Ilium's feet but held his arms.

"You have really done it. Now, you're going outside to die. And all because you listened to this dumb girl," the guardsman spat.

"No!" Avalon yelled and jerked violently against her restraints.

"Good thing this room is sound proof," Viggo said with a look to the guardsman.

The guardsman punched Ilium in the stomach. Ilium yelled out in pain.

"Every time your girlfriend opens her mouth, you will be punched."

Avalon shut her mouth as Ilium grimaced. Avalon's heart sunk as the guard escorted Ilium out of the room, leaving Avalon alone with Viggo.

Chapter Twenty

Skylar and Xin's eyes grew wide with disbelief as they listened to the President's address on the wallscreen in stunned silence.

"I can't believe that Ilium would do such a thing," Skylar said.

"Me either," Xin said.

"But then again. He was hanging around Avalon a lot. I never did trust her," Skylar said.

"Stop it," Xin said.

"Stop what?" Skylar asked with poked out lips.

"Stop being jealous of Avalon. She has done nothing to you, except make the mistake of being nice."

Skylar's mouth fell open. "You don't really mean that do you?"

Xin didn't say anything for a few minutes. The air became stuffy.

"All you have done since we've been in this place is look at Ilium and Kael. You were too blind to see that someone liked you for who you are."

"I won't listen to anymore," Skylar said backing away.

"Yes, you will," he said. "You are enough, just as you are."

No one had said anything like that before to Skylar. She prided herself in her eclectic looks. Her blue spiked pixy hair, her punk rock tastes in music, her oversized earrings. After her brother wasn't allowed in the habitat, she dyed her previously blonde hair blue and her personality slowly became increasingly bitter with each day. If an innocent child couldn't be saved, she didn't want to be either.

Xin closed the gap between them.

"What—what are you doing?" Skylar asked, eyes wide.

"Something I should have done a long time ago," Xin said as he placed his lips gently on hers.

Skylar tried to resist, and at first attempted to push him away, but he just held her tighter. Her eyes closed and she enjoyed the warmth which spread over her body.

She didn't realize it, but she had been self-sabotaging herself. It was hard to sleep at night because all she kept dreaming about was her brother and his face when he learned that she would enter without him. She kept replaying in her head what it must have felt like for those who weren't saved. It was so much easier to be snarky to people than to allow herself to feel. Emotions made you vulnerable and weak. As the last surviving member of her family, she had no choice but to do whatever it took to survive. But deep down, there was still a little girl who dreamt of marrying her prince one day and having six kids. Love was a silly notion she herself had once believed in, before the world went to hell in a hand basket. She was seeking it from all the wrong places, but it was right there in front of her face.

The warmth spread from her stomach to her chest, and radiated all the way down her arms until it made her fingers stretch out. She leaned forward and wrapped her hands around the back of his neck. After a few seconds, Xin withdrew.

"I needed that," she said before clasping her hands around her mouth.

"I know," Xin said with a sly smile.

Skylar playfully hit him. Her cheeks flushed.

Then Xin looked at his smartwatch and shook his head.

"What is it?" Skylar asked.

"Something is wrong. I can't find Avalon."

"Well, track her."

"That's just it," Xin said with a look of concern across his brows. "Avalon's smartwatch isn't picking up."

Ilium was marched through the hallways as people jeered and shouted at him with disgust. Ilium did not hold it against them, however, as he knew they had been misled. The march through the corridor was deliberate, meant to humiliate him and break him down.

Everyone watched on wallscreens as Ilium entered a room where he was fitted into a radiation suit. Ilium tried to appear brave, for Avalon's sake. His face was covered by a full face mask, and he was fitted with a very large cylinder of filtered and compressed air to be carried on his back.

"You are ordered out of the habitat by decree of the President. May you find peace on the other side," the guardsman said.

Ilium often wondered why and how the guardsman could blindly follow the President's commands. And then, he remembered, they were paid the Accipio rates in credits. Money always did have power. Even in the world after impact.

A countdown to open the airlock began.

Ten…..

Nine…..

Eight….

Seven….

Six……

Five….

As his life flashed before his eyes, he contemplated his home life. Or lack thereof. He was raised in an orphanage. However, he was made of strong stock, and due to his intelligence, earned a spot in the habitat.

Four….

Then he thought about how he went to the same high school as Avalon, but she had never noticed him because he was afraid to take a risk and say hello. How she still had not recognized him when she woke up and after all of the time they spent together. The way her hair flowed down her shoulders when she took it out of the ponytail. The way her smile lit up the room and made his heart beat faster while his stomach flipped. Of all the time they could have had together, as friends or more than friends, if he had more time.

Three....

He thought about how she was always the smartest person in the room. How beautiful she was. *What is that crazy psychopath going to do to her?* But it was too late. He was in the airlock. He could not help her from here.

Two....

He thought about the patients who might not receive the cure in time, or at all. The horrible fates they would suffer.

One.....

Ilium tried to regulate his breathing as he thought about what he might see when he stepped outside of the habitat for the first time. Would there be anything left at all? Any ruins?

He would make history as being the first person to see Earth in a hundred years. It was a record he could do without, but a record none the less. At least something good may come of his death.

Ilium's lips formed a straight line. The airlock door opened, evidenced by the grinding noise of metal gears twisting and he was blinded by the flood of sudden light as he held up his hand to shield his eyes.

Avalon was growing tired of listening to Viggo regale her with how much of a genius he was when she jerked at the sound of a knock on the door.

Maybe whoever that is can save me. Avalon breathed a sigh of relief as her heart leapt.

Grabbing a syringe sure to be loaded with something nasty, Viggo looked at a security camera view, and after a slight pause, let the person inside.

"What brings you here today? Are you here to see the fulfillment of my plan in person?" Viggo asked.

"Yes," the figure said as it entered the room.

Avalon's head spun. She knew that voice anywhere. It was Kael. *Of course, he is on it! The formula was found in his smartwatch after all. Blinded by his charm, I wanted to believe it was his father so badly.*

"Excellent," Viggo answered. "I was just about to give Avalon something. But now that you're here, I think it would be better if you administered the shot."

"I think that is a good idea," Kael answered.

Viggo handed Kael the gleaming needle. Kael tapped out the air bubble and walked over to where Avalon sat squirming in her chair. Her eyes widened with fear and she screamed through the duct tape covering her mouth. Terror rose within her chest as she stared at the needle. Her life was going to end today. Right here in this terrible little room, stuck to this chair. All of the effort she and her father took to ensure her a spot in the habitat so she could live was about to be in vain. She would never see Ilium again, or be held by his caring arms.

As Kael grabbed her arm, Avalon made up her mind to cease struggling. She shoved aside the fear and sadness which seized her heart and instead met her ending with a determined look and eyes that could kill. Her fists balled up as Kael pressed the tip of the needle against her olive flesh. Then in one fell swoop, Kael swung around and stuck the needle deep into the jugular vein of Viggo.

"Traitor," Viggo gurgled before he fell to the ground with a thud.

"Let's get you out of here," Kael said to Avalon as he whipped the tape from her mouth.

"You! You!" she kept repeating with harshness in her voice and eyes.

"I just saved your life," he answered as he untied her arms and legs from the chair. "You are welcome."

Avalon punched him square in the jaw.

"Ow!" he yelled, rubbing his cheek, but she could tell it didn't hurt him at all.

"That was for letting Brody die!"

"Fair enough," Kael said. "But I think I deserve a hug or a kiss for rescuing you now."

"You will get neither, and another hit instead if you don't explain what is going on."

"What do you want to know?"

"Everything. But first, what was he about to give me?" Avalon asked.

"A paralyzing agent."

Avalon winced. She didn't want her imagination to travel down that road.

"Why. Why did you save me?" Avalon said, her voice trembling ever so slightly.

"Isn't it obvious?"

"No, it isn't," Avalon hissed. "Whose side are you on?"

"Your side," he answered with a faint smile as he lifted her up from the chair and wrapped one of her arms around his shoulder. With his help, she hobbled towards the door.

"But he called you a traitor. To be a traitor, you must have been on his side."

"A lot of stuff goes on in this habitat that you aren't aware of Avalon. You just have to trust me," Kael said.

"But wait. The formula was found on your smartwatch. The so-called cure for the virus."

"I pretended that I was on Viggo's side. The side of the people who want to destroy the Compatios. But I am not on their side. I don't believe what they believe. I will explain everything else later," Kael urged.

Avalon still didn't trust him. She didn't trust anyone anymore, besides Ilium.

Kael swiped the door open. "Now, go meet up with Xin and Skylar. They are waiting for you outside of your dorm room."

Every step Avalon took hurt, but she nodded her head in agreement. "But, what are you going to do?"

He only offered a wink to her in answer.

Chapter Twenty One

The bright orange orb hanging high in the sky blinded Ilium temporarily. After living underground for so long, it was downright painful to see. He squinted for several seconds and then shut his eyes to give them a rest before taking a single step forward. After a few minutes of this, he opened his eyes for longer stretches of time.

Rich green vegetation and land that once dotted the world was no more. All of the furry animals, large and small, which once darted across the landscape, did so no more. No birds chirped in the sky or flew. In the place of the once green world, full of life from every corner, stood an eerie sea of red. Rusty red rocks, red mountains, and thin wispy red clouds. The cities, ballparks, hotels, restaurants, and other edifices which once loomed large in the skyline were now buried beneath the red sand dunes. No water remained on the desolate surface.

Despite the dismal scene before him, and the abysmal situation which sent him outside, there existed a certain beauty to being outside of the confining walls of the habitat. The walls constantly pressed down, around, and above him, suffocating any possibility for true love, beauty, art, or anything which helped make life, life. Out here, in the open space, he was alive. It didn't matter that he wouldn't be alive long, due to his oxygen tank. He was alive for now.

Looking at the analytics overlay display in his helmet, the temperature was near freezing, but his suit provided plenty of insulation. Radiation levels were almost back to normal, as well. However, it was still above the recommended threshold. When Ilium was living inside of the habitat, he tried not to think about what happened to those left behind. How they might have died. What they may have seen. However, this sight left little to the imagination.

Kael ran down the long corridor to his father's office, pushing people out of the way as he ran.

"Father!" Kael yelled, out of breath as he entered the office.

The President pivoted around from his position of looking at the simulated window which displayed a beautiful green mountain range with rolling white fluffy clouds flying across a bright blue sky.

"Father, you have committed a grave error. You've sent the wrong man to his death!"

"Speak plainly, son," the President said his face frowning.

"Ilium is innocent. Viggo is the one who has been conducting human experiments behind your back."

His father's face fell. "Are you sure of this, son? Do you have proof?"

"Yes. I also don't think he is working alone."

The President frowned. "Son, the Council has always been thorough in their investigations of such matters. IF what you are saying is true, then it is possible other traitors are amongst us," the President said stepping away from the wallscreen and moving closer to his son. "Traitors that are in my inner circle."

"Yes," Kael said.

The President stood closer to Kael until only a few inches were between them. "So I sent an innocent man to his death?"

Kael nodded. "Quickly, Father, you must order him to return to the habitat."

The President hesitated before stating, "I am sorry but I simply cannot do that."

Kael stepped away from his father. He truly beheld his father's face, something he hadn't done in some time. This job had clearly aged him, even in such a short time frame.

"Father, what do you mean you *can't*? The HOPE habitat depends on us correcting mistakes once found."

"I mean that I cannot admit my mistakes in front of the entire habitat like that. Whoever is in charge of orchestrating such a large coup d'état undoubtedly planned all of these events to transpire so I would be embarrassed. As I am. To admit to a mistake would undermine my authority or possibly create civil unrest. As leader of this habitat, I cannot allow this to happen."

Kael did not want to believe his father's stubbornness. He wanted to save the day for Avalon. She wanted Ilium back, and that meant getting him safely returned to HOPE. The father he knew before entering the habitat would have immediately admitted his mistake and made amends. Had the coldness of not seeing the sun done to this him? Had the years of cryosleep affected his brain in ways not measured by the technology?

Regardless of what caused this change, Kael had to persevere. He could not let Avalon down. She needed him. And he needed her. She wasn't a sycophant like the others. She could keep him in line, in check. They all should have perished a long time ago, and many a day he wished he would have despite all of the luxuries which surrounded him. All of the girls. But Avalon was real. There was something about her that he couldn't quite pinpoint, but it made her different from all of the other girls.

"Father, what are you saying?"

The President let out an exasperated puff of breath as a thin firm line formed across his lips. "I mean, he must remain outside."

Ilium continued to walk in the bright heat of the sun. The sky no longer featured rich shades of blue, purple, and green as the sun set. Instead, a brilliant red light shone and cast an inflamed glow upon everything.

He checked the time on his helmet. Thirty-two hours were left. He had been walking for a while, taking shelter under rocks periodically. He needed to find some form of shelter from the bitter cold that was sure to descend upon him at night. The planet, as a result of the substantial loss of atmosphere, could plunge into nights so cold that dry ice would form.

He licked his lips. He had been given one jug of water for his journey. He hesitated to drink from his water jug as he wanted to survive as long as possible, which would require every ounce of water he carried. *I'll wait to take my first sip until right before I go to bed.*

The hours passed, and the stars shone in the night sky as he traveled across the harsh terrain. His helmet displayed he was twenty four miles northwest of the habitat. His pace had slowed tremendously, as now his lungs burned with every breath he took and his limbs felt like they were weighed down by concrete slabs. He paused and peered up to notice the stars which loomed so large and unobscured by the night sky. He once loved the charcoal colored tapestry and all of the brilliant white Milky Way constellations woven throughout, but without any shelter it was foreboding.

He swallowed hard, his thirst beginning to overtake him.

So this is how it all ends, he thought. His side stung like something stabbed him with a knife. His swollen ankles didn't aid matters. *I should have exercised more in the habitat. But of course, they only fed us exactly enough calories to complete our tasks. Never more, never less.*

After all of the time in the habitat of constantly hearing the low hum of electronics, he now found the only noise was that of his own breathing and heartbeat.

Why am I walking? Why am I even trying? What do I hope to find in this desolate place? I might as well sit here and just rest.

As Ilium sat down, his boot scratched against something. It was grey. A seed of hope sprung up in his heart, which he dared not give heed to.

Shelter! His heart soared at the thought. Feverishly, Ilium dug into the dirt and scraped away the red dust from the grey piece of round metal which slightly jutted out from the ground. A large wheel appeared which took all of his strength to turn. After several turns, the hatch door opened.

He cautiously lifted the door up. Tapping his wrist, the suit's flashlight turned on. He had saved it until now, as each use drained the battery. He could detect what appeared to be an underground compound with wood paneled walls, a sofa, and a mattress in the far corner. A couple of open cans with dried food lay in the middle of a table, along with a few weights for exercise. *Whoever lived here must have been pretty flush with cash. To not only have enough funds to build a shelter, but enough money to furnish it warmly.*

"Anybody home?" Ilium yelled.

Since no one answered, Ilium lowered his body unto the ladder and placed his feet on the pegs which led down into the buried shelter. Then he carefully closed the lid before climbing down.

Once he hit the floor, he took note of the size of the bunker. He had about a foot and a half of room above his head, so it wasn't too claustrophobia-inducing. He scanned the room to see if the air was breathable. It was not. His eyes fell to a NBC air filter mounted vertically on the wall which could work if manually turned. After turning the crank for fifteen minutes, he took a small breath of air. He removed his helmet and immediately dry heaved. Quickly, he placed his helmet back on and after several moments began to breathe normally again.

What on earth is that smell!

Ilium shined his light on the table with the rotten can of food. *Could that entire stench come from that?* A small object reflected off of his flashlight in the corner. Turning his light towards the object, he grabbed onto the table to stop dry heaving.

Chapter Twenty Two

Outside of her dorm room, Avalon met up with Skylar and Xin.

"Thank goodness you're back," Xin said.

"Yeah, Kael rescued me from the crazy scientist," she said.

"I can't believe they did that to Ilium," Xin said.

"I know. I don't know how, but we have to figure out a way to rescue him," Avalon said. She noted that Xin was talking far more than usual. Then her eyes turned to an uncharacteristically silent Skylar.

Kael ran up behind Avalon with his chest rising and falling. Kael piped up, "I am working right now to get Ilium back in this habitat. I told my father everything I know about Viggo and his treachery."

"And?" Avalon asked angrily.

"He acknowledges what is happening, and states he will quietly handle the situation."

"So what about Ilium?" Xin asks.

"He refuses to order Ilium back inside, despite my efforts, because he doesn't want to undermine his authority or appear weak before the constituents."

"What?" Avalon yelled, her fists balling up in anger. "The only thing that stands between Ilium's return is your father's *pride?*"

"He is *still* my father," Kael said icily. "Let me work on this."

"No," Avalon said, shaking her head. "You already tried. Meanwhile, every hour we waste in here is another hour Ilium spends out there!" Avalon pointed. "He only has what, thirty-six hours? He has even less than that now!" Avalon shouted, beating her fists on Kael's chest.

Kael let her assault him until she found herself swimming in tears. Then he tried to wrap his arms around her.

"Don't!" she shouted.

"Look, Avalon is right," Xin said as he looked at Kael. "We have tried your way."

Kael looked at Xin." Then what are you suggesting?"

"That you let us try," Xin said as he stood next to Avalon.

Xin waved his wrist over the sensor. He stormed right through the large double doors which separated the rest of the habitat from Accipio Hall and continued walking towards the President's office. Avalon stood right beside him.

"When did you change the access?" Avalon asked.

"I always had access," he answered with a glimmer of mischief in his eyes.

Xin had more sides to him than Avalon knew. She always figured him for the quiet, "always play by the rules" type.

As they rounded a corner, Avalon and Xin spotted two guards standing outside of the President's door. The guard's stood at attention, shoulders squared with alert eyes. Both guards wore their hair the same short style, similar to that of old school Marines. Avalon and Xin ducked into a recessed corner.

"What are we going to do?" Xin asked, pointing at the guards.

"We are going to distract them," Avalon suggested.

"Or we can be more direct," Xin countered.

"Well, which is it?" Avalon whispered.

Xin poked his head around the corner and examined the muscular guards.

"We are going to be direct," he answered.

The two stepped out from the recess and stood in front of the guards who protected the President.

"What are you here for?" a tall guard asked, frowning.

Shorter guard said, "I think I remember this girl. She's the one from the cafeteria."

"Oh yeah...the trouble maker," taller guard said, his face darkening as he smirked.

Avalon swallowed her fear and said, "I need to speak with the President."

The guard studied her for a minute before answering, "Well, I need a million bucks, but you don't see me complaining."

As the two guards chuckled at the horrible joke, Xin balled his fist up. Striking a guard meant two weeks without food. Right before he reared his hand back, Kael walked up behind him and placed a hand on his shoulder.

"Let them through," Kael ordered the two guards.

"But sir, your father has requested that no one be allowed entry."

"Let them through. I won't ask again," Kael demanded in a tone that left no room for negotiation.

Once again, Avalon felt her heart flutter a bit towards Kael. He possessed admirable qualities, but he just wasn't Ilium.

The guards hesitated, but ultimately allowed Avalon, Xin, and Kael inside.

"Son, what are you doing here? And it's great to see you again Avalon," the President asked.

Normally, Avalon would respond back to the President's greeting in kind. It was expected and customary. However, she chose to remain silent lest she say something that would get her locked up.

"These are my *friends*," Kael said giving Xin a sideways glance. "Avalon and Xin are here to convince you that you should allow Ilium to return to the habitat."

The President ignored Xin and looked directly at Kael. "I told you my decision, son. Why have you—"

Avalon cut him off. "Unless you let my friend return to HOPE habitat, you're going to have a mutiny."

The President's eyes widened as he took in this information.

"What did you say?" the President asked as he stepped closer to Avalon. Xin stepped in front of Avalon in a protective gesture. Strangely, Avalon did not feel threatened by the President, though she knew she should. Kael stood to the side, careful not to appear to take sides.

"With all due respect, *sir*," Avalon said allowing the sarcasm to drip from the word like sap from a tree, "I have reason to believe that someone is already threatening not only your life, and your control, but potentially the lives of everyone on board. I don't know exactly who is behind these events, but I think the first way you could remedy this situation is by letting Ilium return to the habitat."

The President cocked his head to the side. "Remind me why I should do this again?"

"Because it's the right thing to do," Avalon answered. "You know my father voted for you, more than one hundred years ago. He said you stood for something. I wonder if you still do today."

The President bristled at her comment as he stepped over to his wallscreen. He fixated on the portrait on his desk of his wife, the one he had to leave behind when he entered the habitat.

Avalon knew she shouldn't provoke the President. Yet, the words kept spewing from her mouth in her desperation.

"You know, you two barging into my office could be considered a threat. A threat to our survival. I could throw *both* of you out of the habitat," he threatened.

At this, Kael spoke. "Father will think about your wishes overnight," he said giving his father a glance. The President said nothing in the affirmative, but he didn't say no either.

"But Ilium only has so many hours left!" Avalon shouted, unable to help herself.

Kael winced at how much she cared for Ilium. However, he could not blame her. People often fell for those with whom they were in close proximity. How he longed to have someone who would stand up for him, fight for him, like that.

"Enough. I will think about this overnight." The President said. "I know exactly how many hours he has left." He paused. "Guards, usher them out. And another thing— a word to anyone about what has been discussed in this room and the deal is off."

Xin, Avalon, and Kael were ushered out of the room.

Then the President turned to the guard inside of the room and said, "Bring me Viggo."

The security guard nodded his head and returned to the lab.

Viggo was still slumped over on the floor but aware.

"What are you doing here?" Viggo managed to say.

"I am here to take you to the President," the large security guard said as he took one of Viggo's wrists and handcuffed him.

"For what?" Viggo said with wide eyes.

"Treason."

Viggo ambled with the guard to the President's office.

The guard threw Viggo on the President's couch. The President walked over to Viggo and stood above him as he spoke.

"What have you done? Who do you really work for?" the President inquired.

"What makes you think I work for anyone?" Viggo spat.

The President sighed. "The fact you were always a follower, Viggo, not a leader."

Viggo rolled his eyes.

"I have ways of making you tell me what I want to know. You of all people realize this, as you designed the drug yourself." The President stated. "Your duty was to help us develop better plants and improve life in this habitat. Now, I uncover that you weren't working on fixing our problems—you were creating *new* problems."

The President studied Viggo's face. But it was indecipherable. He continued to speak, "You were only concerned about yourself. I also know that your experiments resulted in the deaths of the lives we were entrusted with."

Viggo did not look the President in the face but instead looked at the wall.

"Look at me, or I will make you look at me," the President said.

After Viggo's continued refusal, the President ordered, "Send him to the holding cell."

As the guard grabbed Viggo's arm and lifted him off of the couch, he yelled, "You think you're safe. That everyone is loyal to you. But you don't know. Many of us disagree with you. At the proper time, we'll show ourselves, and it will be your head."

"Out with him," the President calmly stated. "And Viggo, it is by my mercy that I am letting you live. You *will* tell me everything you know."

The security guards ushered Viggo out of the room.

I don't know what I expected to find. It makes sense. Of course, it would only be bones. It has been over a century, Ilium thought.

The object was a small wristwatch which belonged to what he presumed was the father. He counted four skeletal remains with tattered clothes attached. A father, mother, and one girl. *They didn't last long, as the girl did not develop into a woman, judging by the skeleton.* In a corner were stacks of books and board games, something considered ancient. The bunker had a small fridge, wood stove, and a restroom and shower area partially hidden by a Japanese folding privacy screen.

Ilium showed respect before mooching off of their shelter by pausing to say a small prayer. His tongue was dry, so he took a swig of his water bottle. Surveying the room some more, two mattresses and a pile of blankets sat in a corner. *Probably crawling with things I don't want to think about.* Still, he took a chance, and after knocking the dirt and grime from the mattress, lay across pulling one of the blankets on top of him. He stared up at the ceiling for a long time.

His mind drifted to when he and Avalon hugged. He had not received a hug like that since entering the orphanage. His mom gave hugs like that— hugs that radiated the warmth of the person giving them. In the embrace, his muscles loosened from the rigidity he had developed from being forced to defend himself against the world all of those years, how small and dainty Avalon was in his arms, and a strong desire to protect her from all of the bad the world could offer. It was not something that he was conscious of, it happened naturally and involuntarily. No matter what happened to them, or who she chose to date in the future, he would always be her protector and comforter. He would do his best to ensure no harm came to her in any way.

Then a wave of shame hit him as he recalled how harm was being inflicted upon her right now, at the hands of Viggo. His fists balled up, but he eventually fell asleep.

Chapter Twenty Three

Sleep did not come easily to Avalon that night. She missed Ilium deeply. The sunshine in her life had left her grasping in the dark. The cadence of his laughter, the way he tousled his hair when in deep thought, and how his face lit up in her presence were memories which she held on to for dear life. Living in the habitat without Ilium was not living, it was surviving.

I miss him so much. At first, it was more of a friendship, but now it has become so much more.

Chances are slim that he is still alive, much less that he will return in one piece. Who knows what dangers lie outside? How will seeing all that destruction affect him?

Avalon could wait no longer for the President to make his decision. Her head turned at the sound of a knock on her door. She slid her legs out of her capsule bed and hopped down to the ground.

Kael. What is he doing here?

"What do you want?" she asked through the door.

"For you to open the door."

Avalon unlocked the door, allowing Kael to swipe into her dorm.

Kael stopped and looked at her face which was red and puffy.

"What about Ilium? What is your father thinking?" Avalon asked.

Kael's face fell. "I don't understand him myself. He keeps saying that he won't do it."

"Well, I can't just sit here and let Ilium die. You must understand that," Avalon said.

Kael took a long steady breath before saying, "I do."

Kael eyed Avalon before adding, "Please, whatever you're planning, be safe."

"Is that concern I detect in your voice?" Avalon asked mockingly.

Kael took a step closer. "Yes. Before you awoke in the habitat, my life was largely mundane and routine. Since you woke up, my life has been nothing but an adventure. I know you think Accipios have it made— and we do as far as creature comforts go, but all of this comes with huge responsibility."

He took another step until they were mere inches apart. "You see, I was actually relieved when Match Day matched me with you. I didn't want a predictable life with Elena. I want a crazy one with you," he said.

249

Avalon could barely process the words coming out of his mouth. At one time, she would have been delighted to hear those words, but not now. As she opened her mouth to speak, his lips fell on hers and engulfed her in a passionate kiss.

Despite the passion of his kiss, her body did not come alive. Avalon gently withdrew her lips and shook her head.

That's when she understood. Kael could provide safety, money, and food. But, Ilium could provide his whole heart.

"I understand," Kael said. He straightened his shoulders and returned to the regal air he normally displayed to others.

A look of annoyance and hardness was in his eyes before he swiped his wrist and left the room.

Anger rippled through her body again as she imagined Ilium running out of oxygen. All alone.

I've lost too much to this asteroid. My father. My family. Brody. My normal life. I can't afford to lose Ilium too. If I have to stay awake worrying about Ilium, then the President will too.

The President jolted awake as an alarm went off in his chamber at 0400 in the morning.

"What is it?" he yelled, kicking the sheets off of him as his feet hit the cold floor. A chill climbed up his spine.

"The systems are crashing, sir!" someone on the night shift said on his wallscreen.

"What systems?"

"Several systems critical to the habitat, sir. They appear to be working, but I am not sure because the lights are blinking on and off on the oxygenator—does that mean it's working or it's not working?"

The President called upon several Accipios for assistance. However, they were unable to resolve the situation. While frustrated, and pacing the floor, he received a videomessage from Avalon Adams.

"Hello, Mr. President," Avalon said with a smirk.

The President's eyes were a bit bloodshot. "It is you... isn't it?"

"It isn't wholly me. But yes. I am demonstrating that without us, this whole habitat could suffer just like without Ilium, I am suffering. Speaking of, have you had time to make up your mind yet about Ilium?"

A tiny vein on the President's temple began to pulse. His face turned crimson. "I could get rid of you. With or without the recommendation of the Council."

"Yes, you could," Avalon answered. "But you won't. Because you *need* us. So enough of this chitchat. Give me what I want."

The President glared at her, but then, with a sigh of frustration, the President agreed to return Ilium to the habitat and reinstate his civil rights in full. Avalon was filled with joy and thanked the President. She messaged Xin to let him know the good news as well.

The President waited till breakfast time the next morning to issue an announcement via the wallscreen.

"Good morning, everyone. I have an announcement to make."

Everyone turned to face the wallscreen no matter what they were previously engaged in.

"I received ill intelligence the other day on the matter of who was poisoning us. It turned out not to be Ilium after all."

Gasps erupted throughout the habitat.

"Don't worry. I've ordered Ilium to return to the habitat, and his rights will be reinstated in full. Meanwhile, I have also fired the one responsible for this false intelligence."

That last part is not true.

"Carry on, and remember if you see anything out of the ordinary to report it to the security guards."

Avalon ran to the airlock to wait for Ilium's return.

That same morning, Ilium woke up in total darkness. His heart beat faster, as humans aren't meant to be in darkness. Touching his wrist to activate the flashlight, his eyes slowly adjusted to the slim sliver of light as he took a swig of water from his jug. Rising from the cold hard floor, Ilium's back ached. The hunger inside of him grew as his stomach begged for mercy.

There has to be water here. Sure, the food has all gone stale, but water...water would last. Surely these people could not have survived so long without it.

Ilium ran his hands along the smooth walls of the compound, desperately searching for anything odd or out of place.

Why would they hide the water? Were they expecting people to raid this place?

Six planks were a slightly different shade than the others. He quickly tore at the planks and found a large 55-gallon drum full of water.

Yes! Ilium unscrewed his water canteen lid and began refilling it from the tap on the bottom of the water drum.

I can survive, he thought for the first time since leaving the habitat as he sipped the water. He tried not to sip it too fast, as that would make him sick and dehydrated again.

Now, all I have to find is some food. Despite the fact I haven't seen anything, doesn't mean nothing is out there. Maybe some small plant around here survived.

Just as hope swelled in his heart, his helmet comm crackled.

"Come," a security guard instructed on his comm unit inside his helmet.

"What?" Ilium said as he glanced down at his oxygen level which was at 30%. He thought maybe he had begun to hallucinate.

"Come back," the voice said, a little bit clearer than before. *Was this voice playing a trick with him?*

"You have been pardoned. Please return immediately," the voice stated clearly.

Ilium's heart leapt with joy until his oxygen tank revealed he only had four hours to walk twenty four miles.

Chapter Twenty Four

Ilium's whole body became stronger, invigorated by the opportunity to reunite with Avalon again. But his oxygen levels were a problem. He simply did not have enough to reach the habitat in time. *Should I go? Or should I stay?* He could technically remain in the habitat if he found adequate food sources. Or, he could use the last of his oxygen and at least make an attempt to reunite with Avalon again.

At the thought of Avalon, Ilium practically leapt up the bunker's ladder and unlocked the hatch to return to the surface. He took one big breath as he sprinted back towards the mountain which lay in the distance like a red camel's hump, praying his oxygen would last. However, it was increasingly difficult to see as sandstorms brought bright orange dust which hit his helmet obscuring his vision. His footsteps were erased as soon as he made them. Luckily, his suit's tracker helped him to navigate his way.

Ilium began to falter. So close, so close. He fell down to the ground with a thud. Turning over on his back so he could see the sky before he died, a shape in the form of a two-legged animal moved towards him.

Must be a hallucination. I am told that's part of the death process. His breathing slowed and slowed as the shape took on the form of a man. As the man came nearer, he became even more certain that it was indeed a man. The man loomed large over him, dark complexioned, barefoot and with dirty tattered clothes. A large scar ran across his face from his forehead to his chin.

The scar appeared to follow a Lichtenberg pattern, suggesting the man may have been struck by lightning.

Grasping his chest, darkness clouded his vision and the world went silent as Ilium blacked out.

Lights. Lots of brilliant light and a lightweight feeling. Colors are supernaturally bright and brilliant. Effervescent bubbles float around in all shapes and sizes. It's beautiful.

This man—where did he come from? And why is he here? I feel as though I am being carried. I am gasping, gasping. Struggling to breathe. Ow—it hurts as my lungs fill with oxygen again. I can breathe. He removes his hands from my chest. His eyes are gold—not just amber brown but truly golden in color. I feel stronger than before. Where am I? This looks like the inside of a large cave. How did I get here? I thought before you die, you were supposed to see your loved ones flash before your eyes. This man is not my loved one. I should be seeing my parents. Or

Avalon. What is he giving me to drink? No, I don't want it. His eyes are scaring me, so I drink it. Now I feel sleepy again.

When Ilium opened his eyes again, he was lying flat on his back. Slowly, he stood up.

What just happened? Was that real? Did I just pass out?

He could breathe fine now.

I don't know what just happened, but I have to hurry up.

He began to sprint and before long he was only a few feet from the habitat. The hatch door loomed large and beautiful before him. It represented shelter. It represented Avalon. His heart thudded rapidly in his chest as the hatch door slowly opened.

No sooner than he stepped into the airlock, the AI turned on a UV light to conduct an analysis on him.

"Welcome back, Ilium. Proceeding to scan for radiation and other environmental contaminants." After a few moments of the light dancing across his suit, the AI said, "Scan complete. Please step into the side room for sterilization."

Ilium stepped into a side room where his suit was sterilized with various chemicals. As it was sprayed, he closed his eyes. He was so thankful to be back inside. To no longer have to ration his water. To be able to breathe freely. Still, something happened out there. Something he couldn't explain.

The spray stream stopped. "You may remove your outer suit now and re-enter the habitat," the AI announced.

Avalon waited impatiently for Ilium. *Will he feel the same way for me or will he still have feelings for Raleigh?* But then as soon as he exited the airlock, her fears were relieved as her heart swelled at his sight. Strange electricity came over her whole body as she inhaled his scent in the tender embrace she gave him. They slowly broke away from each other, and his hand was holding hers. She did not move away.

"Thank goodness, you're back! We were worried sick about you!" Avalon said.

Ilium thought more time had passed than did, and when he snuck a peek at his oxygen levels, it read zero.

"Let's get you settled," she said, escorting him to his dorm.

Viggo sat in his holding cell. He did not mind his new environment. The cold floor, grey walls, overall silence, and lack of windows matched his heart.

The guard passed Viggo his tray of dinner around 1700 that night. However, Viggo was in no mood to eat. He was in the mood for revenge. So his food sat in the corner, untouched.

I am not the bad guy here. I am trying to save humanity. The best of humanity. Purify the race. There is no need to save the inferior! So why not use them? Why would a farmer plant inferior seeds if he could plant seeds guaranteed to yield delicious ripe fruit? The President didn't have the guts to make the hard choices. The choices necessary for our survival.

At first, I utilized a few computer models which were designed to simulate rat and mice models. But the scale wasn't sufficient. There weren't enough data points. I needed realistic data, more data. Data I could only accurately acquire from a human, not a computer model, Viggo thought.

Around midnight, way past normal visiting hours, a security guard unlocked the door to Viggo's cell.

"What is going on?" Viggo asked with wide eyes. "I've never heard of anyone being sentenced in the middle of the night."

"No, you aren't being sentenced. You have a visitor," the security guard answered as he led Viggo to a visitation area booth. Clear Plexiglas stood between him and the visitor on the other side.

Viggo's face lit up.

"Thank you for gracing me with your presence!" Viggo said. After a moment, he added, "I am so sorry I failed you. However, I did *not* tell the President anything about you."

"Very good. I knew you wouldn't. You are very loyal," the visitor reassured.

"Thank you, your grace. You are most gracious," Viggo said with relief.

"Don't speak of it. You've served me well."

"The world will remember me won't they? I will be famous like you said?" Viggo asked.

"Famous," the figure repeated. "By the way, I brought you some bread. I had to pay the guard extra for this," the cloaked figure said handing him some bread through a small hole in the glass.

"Thank you," Viggo said, biting off a piece of bread and quickly chewing it. "You wouldn't believe the food they serve to prisoners here. Absolutely disgusting. I *almost* feel sorry for the lower classes."

"Are our final plans in order?" The figure asked.

"Yes. Everything is just as you said. The President does not suspect a thing."

"Continue to eat. Your reward will be even greater if you pull this off," the figure said, walking away.

Once Ilium returned to his dorm, Avalon brought him some warm soup. Avalon had never entered his dorm before.

He was allowed to live alone until the full 5000 members awakened as courtesy for being the physician. What Avalon didn't know was what a penchant he had for ancient books and movies.

Ilium had an excellent drawing ability, and his room was lined with pictures of elves and beings from the Lord of the Rings and intricate maps of make-believe worlds. Her fingers ran across the covers of some old books. *He must have smuggled these in undetected somehow. Ilium, you sly dog.* Avalon opened the dusty books, letting out a plume of dust into the air. She sniffled a few times and ran her hands across the wrinkled yellow pages. Nothing could compare to the unique feel of ancient paper.

His appearance had changed slightly since he returned. His bright eyes still remained, but the rest of his appearance bore little to the boyish mid-westerner Avalon had first met. Where his face was once a tad pudgy, now stood sharp lines.

Ilium chuckled. "Isn't this interesting. Now *you* are feeding me."

Avalon smiled. Inside, Ilium was the same as always. "I thought I'd lost you. Forever," her voice shook as she said the word forever.

Ilium stood up and took her hands into his. He gingerly placed his hands around her slender waist. Then he tilted her chin, which was pointing down, up towards his face. Avalon was once again taken aback by how the boyish Ilium had been replaced with a more chiseled version. Gently, he removed a strand of hair which slipped from her ponytail and placed it behind her ear. Then he leaned in and gave her a soft kiss on her cheek.

"You don't ever have to worry about that again."

Avalon tried to hide her disappointment that the kiss had not landed on her lips and instead began to pepper him with questions. "So tell me, what was it like out there? Is it totally desolate like my father projected? Or is there some tiny piece of green that managed to survive?"

Ilium lowered his eyes. "Everything is destroyed. There is nothing but a sea of red dust. I didn't see a speck of water anywhere or any trees. I honestly don't know if we can terraform." After he said that, once again, the image of the dark complexioned man came to his mind. Ilium considered whether or not to tell

Avalon about his strange encounter with the man on the outside, but instead, he chalked it up to a hallucination as a result of a near-death experience and decided to keep it to himself.

"I know it looks bad. But my father predicted that the air should at least be breathable by the time the countdown clock finishes. I am sure that given enough time, we can make it work outside," Avalon said.

Avalon hugged Ilium, which he returned. Still, he was slightly unsettled that he hallucinated a strange man instead of life at the orphanage, or Avalon.

"Rest up," she said, about to swipe her wrist across the door. That's when Ilium grabbed her wrist softly from behind and turned her towards him. Avalon's body buzzed with electricity and warmth as she inhaled Ilium's scent. Wrapped in his embrace, she listened to his heartbeat like it was the hottest soundtrack of the summer.

"You were what I thought about when I was outside. When I thought I was going to die. Every step I took, I took for you," Ilium said as he pressed his lips against Avalon's.

That's when Avalon's smartwatch buzzed.

"Who is it?" Ilium asked with irritation.

Avalon paused. "Brody."

Chapter Twenty Five

Ilium and Avalon stared at the smartwatch in disbelief.

"How could it be?" Avalon asked.

"Answer it," Ilium said without hesitation.

Avalon answered the phone.

"Hey, guys! What's happening?" a voice said.

Avalon shook. She knew the voice was Brody's. Still it could be a sick trick played by Viggo. *Trust no one.*

"Fine. How are you?" she asked.

"Man, I am much better now I am over this virus thing. You guys wouldn't *believe* what happened to me! Ilium gave me some shot, which he thought would make me better, but it didn't help. So a few hours later, I flatlined."

"That must have been a terrible experience," Avalon said calmly.

"Not really. Because the weirdest part is I woke up."

"What do you mean, you woke up?" Ilium asked.

"I woke up. After waking up, I feel super strong. I tried it out, and I can lift stuff I could never dream of before."

Avalon wanted to hang up the phone, sure it was some bot Viggo programmed to talk to her realistically until then she remembered Dexter. Dexter said the virus killed him. But then he mutated. He became something else. Could this be the case also with Brody?

"Brody, where are you? We want to meet you?" Avalon asked.

"I am right outside guys," Brody answered.

Avalon looked at Ilium. Ilium nodded his head to say it was all right to open the door, while he hid by the side, ready to pounce if anything should happen.

Avalon opened the door. Broad shoulders and an even broader smile greeted her. It was definitely Brody.

"Brody!" Avalon screamed as she hugged him. Instantly, all of her feelings of unease disappeared.

However, Ilium wasn't so sure. He stood still in the corner and merely watched, his gaze guarded and analytical.

"What's the matter Ilium? Don't recognize me?"

Ilium didn't move a muscle.

"It's him," Avalon said, hoping Ilium would say something back to Brody.

"Darn right, it's me! Who else could it be?" Brody chuckled.

"Anyone," Ilium answered through clenched teeth.

Brody looked dead at Ilium. "You have a right to be cautious. Some weird, freaky, unpleasant stuff has been going on in this place."

Ilium nodded in acknowledgment.

"I really appreciate how hard you two worked trying to save me from the virus too. I hate it didn't work, as I can tell it caused you stress. But something else happened instead. Something wonderful. And as a result, I am stronger now. Stronger than I ever was before."

Avalon nodded her head, but Ilium wasn't so convinced.

"Who else knows you're alive now?" Ilium asked.

"Nobody. I came straight to you guys."

"Good," Avalon said. "Keep it that way for now."

"Where do I go?" he asked.

Avalon and Ilium exchanged glances. "The storage room for now."

Brody nodded. "We'll let you know when it's safe to let others know," Avalon said.

Around 1200 hours, the President sent a wallscreen message throughout the habitat calling for everyone to assemble in the cafeteria for Viggo's sentencing. In lieu of his hurried decision with Ilium, the President wanted to follow the rulebook with Viggo.

Everyone obliged, as that was around normal lunch times, and everyone obeyed the President.

"I am hungry, so I hope he gets this over with," Skylar said.

Avalon rolled her eyes as she entered the cafeteria. Skylar was begging for someone to just punch her in the face and shut her up. But Avalon's excitement over Brody overwhelmed Skylar's ability to get under her skin.

The room had been rearranged to better resemble a courtroom setting. The President sat behind a large wooden desk a few yards in front of Viggo. The jury, as it were, consisted of the six Council members who sat to the side of the President. The President ordered everyone to sit down and serve as witnesses to the trial.

Viggo stood before the President to hear his sentencing. Two guards flanked his sides in case he tried anything, despite his hands and feet being shackled.

In the habitat, defense attorneys did not exist. Each individual represented themselves. However, the rule of innocent until proven guilty still prevailed.

"Viggo. You have been charged with committing multiple atrocious acts against the members of this habitat. Tell me, what do you plea?" The President asked.

"Not guilty."

"I figured you would say that although I hoped you would plead guilty so I might exercise mercy upon you. Despite everything, you truly were a brilliant scientist."

"Thank you. I would just like to say that one day you all will realize my greatness. I am not guilty of maliciously killing anyone. What I did was all for the betterment of our species. Some people had to be sacrificed for the greater good of the many. This is an unfortunate truth. However, to categorize me as a monster is a heinous malapropism. I know you're going to cast me out, no matter what I say. But I do want to leave you with the words of Niccolo Machiavelli."

The President listened in silence.

"There is nothing more difficult, to take in hand, more perilous to conduct, or more uncertain in its success, than to take the lead in the introduction of a new order of things."

Silence followed briefly before someone yelled, "Boo!"

The President allowed the audience to continue booing for a minute before he waved his hands in the air to silence them.

"By the power vested in me as President of this habitat, you, Viggo, are sentenced to expulsion from the habitat for your repeated and egregious cri—"

The entire habitat began to shake, cutting off The President mid-sentence.

Avalon's eyes widened with horror as she stared at Viggo, who only smirked as the second shake caused him to fall to his knees.

"You did this!" she yelled.

"Yes, I did. I planted a series of explosives which are currently detonating!"

Avalon opened her mouth to speak again when she was deafened by the sound of another explosion. Several ceiling tiles crashed to the ground while exposed air ducts dangled hazardously. The lights flickered off and on. Shards of metal flew towards Avalon, who shielded her face with her arm. Her arm stung as blood trickled from it and tiny shards of metal stuck in her hair, lightly pricking her scalp.

Viggo ran to the exit, but Avalon tried to block him despite her injury. Ilium beat her to the punch and rammed into him full force. Ilium sat on top of Viggo, wrapping his legs around the latter's midsection, pinning him down to the ground. Viggo squirmed to get loose as Ilium fought to hold his arms down. Viggo continued to bite and buck against him.

"Are you okay?" Ilium asked Avalon.

"Yeah, just a cut on my arm," she replied.

A guard yelled out, "Children of Ash" before rushing towards Ilium when Avalon spotted a piece of fallen metal swinging low like a pendulum from the ceiling. Grabbing it, she ran towards the guard, her boots crunching on shattered metal and glass, and slammed it as hard as she could into the back of the guard's skull.

"Thanks," Ilium said without taking his eyes or arms off of Viggo.

Avalon nodded, despite her lightheaded sensation. She tore at her left pants leg and ripped it. Wrapping a piece of it around her arm to stop the bleeding.

Another explosion erupted, and Viggo used the shock to arch his back and push off from underneath Ilium. Avalon ran towards Viggo and swung the metal she held as hard as she could.

It missed.

Viggo darted past Ilium and ran through the cafeteria door. Ilium and Avalon followed him, but Viggo had already entered the air lock. Viggo waved goodbye and without any proper suiting stepped outside. *Viggo is crazier than I realized.*

Avalon caught her breath and looked at Ilium as the habitat floor kept quaking.

"The explosions," she yelled over the deafening noise, "I think they wiped out the oxygen generator."

"That's not the only thing they wiped out," Ilium yelled as several warning lights flickered and the AI kept saying, "Warning. Oxygen levels low. Warning, Water levels low. Warning, Atmosphere rapidly changing inside."

Avalon and Ilium ran back to the cafeteria. Chaos abounded as people hunched under tables and bled out from their wounds.

"What on earth are we going to do?" Avalon asked Ilium with tears in her eyes.

The President walked over to her and held her. Avalon shook away from the President.

"Don't you dare touch me! This is all your fault! All of this is your fault. If you had only been more observant. You were the one who let that crazy Viggo in the habitat when it should have been my father!" she yelled.

"That is true. But now, allow me to control the people. You have shouldered a responsibility which wasn't yours."

"Because you failed to shoulder it," Avalon spat.

"I admit.... I've failed you in the past. But you *must* trust me now," he said.

"Trust you? After all of these innocent people died, whose deaths could have been prevented if you had been more vigilant?" Avalon screams. "Those in the cryochambers who will never awaken? Those who were taken for experiments like Michelle?"

The President's eyes flickered with anger but gave way to sorrow.

Avalon clenched her jaw. She had more to say but chose not to because her words were having an effect on him. Despite her feelings towards him, he possessed some undeniable tactical survival techniques due to his age alone. A few minutes passed as everyone held their breath to see if another explosive was going to go off.

It didn't.

Her shoulders slowly relaxed. But then she remembered something. *Why was that guard about to strike Ilium? Viggo kept saying he wasn't alone......Since he was in the holding cell for so long, who helped to plant the bombs?*

Out of the corner of her eye, Avalon began scanning the room for culprits. Whoever it was, would have probably tried to leave the room, or they would not be as shocked as the others. Avalon carefully glanced at Skylar. She was in a corner sobbing, so it wasn't her. Next, she looked at Raleigh, who was in obvious shock. Plus, it just didn't fit her profile. Her mind flew to Kael, but he wouldn't do such a thing, not after saving her from Viggo and helping to get Ilium back inside. *No...it has to be.* Her eyebrows lifted as she locked eyes with

Elena. Normally cool and collected, Elena was sweaty. Abnormally so.

As they locked eyes, Elena started to open her mouth but began to run instead. One of the good guards tried to grab her arm, but they weren't fast enough. Elena fell to the ground.

To her shock, Dexter appeared in the room, struck her in a pressure point and then disappeared.

"Good job Avalon," the President said.

"It wasn't me. It was Dexter," Avalon said.

"Dexter," various voices repeated.

"I will explain later," Avalon said as she rushed to Elena.

Avalon shook her awake. "Elena? Why would you help Viggo? Did you know what he was doing?"

Elena maintained a hard face. Full of envy and vengeance. "You wouldn't understand. All of your life people have said you were special, pretty, etc. Some of us weren't told that, despite our talents. Viggo offered to help change that. To give me something to make me special. I thought Kael would..." her bottom lip trembled.

"No, Elena. I won't ever take you back. Especially after this," Kael said.

Elena's face darkened.

"Please, tell us more," Avalon pleaded.

But Elena remained silent.

The Council member who did all the speaking caused Elena's smartwatch to send a small pulse of pain to her. As her face contorted, Avalon looked at the Council member and shook her head.

"Let's not use force. Either she tells or she doesn't," Avalon said.

The Council member said nothing while quietly contemplating whether or not to continue with another pain cycle. Then he lowered his hand to his side.

One shot was enough as Elena opened her mouth to speak again. "We are called the Children of the Ash, and Viggo promised that I would be special one day," and then Elena's eyes closed as she drifted asleep.

"Great. Just great," Ilium said, shaking his head.

One of the guards placed cuffs around Elena's arms.

"Anyone else involved with Viggo, Elena or these Children of the Ash?"

No one else moved.

Avalon turned to Ilium with wide eyes. "Brody!"

Chapter Twenty Six

The ventilation systems were shut down. Everyone stood still in the eerie silence that followed the violent quakes. The clock still had seven months left before the atmosphere outside would be deemed safe to breathe via its algorithms. Yet, the habitat was completely and utterly destroyed.

"I am going to go get him," Ilium said.

"No, it's too dangerous!" Avalon said.

"Brody is dead! What are you two talking about?" Xin and Skylar asked.

"He is not dead. He is alive," Avalon said. A hush fell over the habitat.

"How can that be?" Skylar asked.

"There is no time for that now. Just go!" Avalon yelled. But no sooner than she ordered Ilium to go,

Brody came. People gasped. Rocks and debris were lodged in his hair.

"Thank goodness you're all right!" Avalon said as she ran to hug him.

"Yeah. I told you I was strong," he said with a smile. Despite all of the debris in his hair and his torn clothes, not a scratch was on him.

"Somebody needs to explain to us what the blue blazes is going on!" someone shouted.

That snapped Avalon back to the present situation.

"There will be time to explain a bunch of things. I promise. I will explain all of the mysterious events which have been plaguing us. But right now, we must evacuate."

Chaos erupted as people shouted in protest.

"Listen! We have no choice. The emergency generator is failing. Only 30% of the lights are on right now. Our life support systems are failing. We must evacuate the habitat," Avalon announced.

"But it's unsafe!" someone yelled.

"We can fix it!" another yelled.

Avalon shook her head. "It's too much to fix in too little of time. Without our systems working, we are doomed to die. The clock only had seven months left. We are going to have to take a chance."

"We don't have to listen to you!" An Accipio yelled. Brody stood in front of the Accipio and cracked his knuckles from side to side. Brody's face was red and his eyes were full of bloodlust.

"Say that again?" Brody asked.

The Accipio flushed crimson but did not repeat his statement.

"Look, we have to leave. The oxygen turbines are permanently destroyed. We have no other choice *but* to go outside," Avalon asserted.

"We'll need to gather guns, flashlights, food, and anything else you think we'll need for the outside," the President opined to the group. No one moved. He no longer controlled them.

Avalon nodded her head. "Yes, everyone listen to the President. Gather anything and everything you think we'll need for the outside. Temperatures are extremely cold. We need to gather our tent packs as well and several first aid kits. Remember your Match Day partner to ensure we don't leave anyone behind."

People gathered several supplies, including a paper copy of a map of the old Earth. Everyone had a tent pack, which was a large backpack with first aid kits, matches, knives, water canteens, MRE packs, and a tent.

"Who will go outside first?" a Compatio asked.

"The President should go first since I believe he got us into this mess," another Compatio shouted.

The habitat shook again.

"What is that?" Avalon shouted.

"Aftershocks. After the initial bombs were set off, it probably created a system of disturbance which we are currently feeling," Ilium answered.

Avalon ducked under a table and Ilium followed, covering her with his body. After a couple of minutes, the shaking stopped. Ilium grabbed her hand and said,

"We aren't waiting for this thing to collapse on us. We are getting the hell out of here!"

Stunned by this move by Ilium and yet simultaneously thrilled, Avalon inhaled a large breath and placed her hand on the large airlock wheel. This was the moment everyone in the habitat had been waiting for their whole lives. To finally go outside. Only they never expected for it to happen it like this. Either she would survive on the outside, or she would not. Ilium's breath warmed her neck as he stood right behind her, giving her constant moral support. She had to be strong for the people. Metal turned against metal as the door opened, leaving only one door in her way to the outside. She hesitated for a moment, hoping no one saw the beads of perspiration which darted her forehead and praying that her hands weren't too slippery from sweat to open the door.

The door opened, and Avalon shielded her eyes with her hands for a moment before they adjusted to the bright light. The air was cold and dry as it hit against her face and cheeks. Her nose was assaulted by the odor of sulfur. However, she inhaled deeply and let it wash over her lungs. Ilium grabbed her hand and she closed her eyes as she relished the sensation she was experiencing.

Everyone smiled and cheered, enjoying the sun upon their faces for the first time in ages. The sun was bright, but it was right, natural, to be outside. It was startling at the same time, as nothing green grew outside anymore. A sea of nothing but red stretched as far as the eye could see, just as Ilium had described it to her earlier. It took a moment for all of her senses to adjust to everything around her. Like a seedling growing towards the light from which it finds nourishment.

How are we going to rebuild? They had plans to rebuild. They just didn't expect to use them this soon.

"Can you believe it?" Avalon said, looking into Ilium's eyes which, for the first time in a long while, only held contentment in them.

"Yes, but justice hasn't truly been served. I mean Viggo is still alive out there somewhere," Ilium said.

"Yes, but we have Elena and we can question her about this Children of Ash," Avalon stated.

"With a name like that, that means there are many of them. This means there are others amongst us who are dangerous."

Avalon shivered as a cold gust of wind struck her dead on. "That's true. But for now, let's not worry about that," Avalon said as she closed her eyes and took in a deep breath of air. Despite all of the things which happened in the habitat, out here, they could start anew. Sure Viggo was somewhere out there, but it was more than a thousand people to his one. They could survive. They could thrive.

Slowly, Avalon opened her eyes and looked out over the horizon. With a smile, she saw the awe she held for the world outside matched by her friends faces.

"Okay, guys. I know we are all in awe of everything around here, but we need to pitch our tents."

A chorus of sighs rung out amongst the crowd.

"We all know dust storms are coming. We don't want to be caught up in one when they hit," she added.

Brody and some others unzipped their backpacks and started the process of pitching tents.

"Make no mistake. We don't plan on stopping here but for a night. We must continue until we find an area we can mine for water. Water has to be underground somewhere."

Various people nodded their heads and others continued to chat amongst themselves. Just being out in the open, relaxed people. It was visible on their faces and their body language.

But behind her someone began to cough. At first it was just a small cough, like from the common cold. Then it progressed until it sounded as though they were choking. Avalon raced towards them when she noticed the sound of coughing increased as all around her, the members of the group began to cough, one by one, as a rotten stench filled her nose. Sores appeared across the member's arms, mouths, and legs. Burnt. Flesh. Avalon swiveled her head and noticed someone else cough up blood. It wasn't long before a sea of bodies stretched across the ground.

Avalon screamed. Images which were not her own filled her mind. They belonged to someone else, yet she was receiving them like a radio receiving channels. These images belonged to a male and they were horrific. Avalon fell to the ground. Avalon's mind was also flooded with memories of the same man with a young child. A young child that looked a lot like her. *No, this was me! Memories of me laughing on the playground, with cookie dough on my face. How could this man have memories of me? As a child at that.*

This same man injected an odd substance into his veins. His body convulsed, and shook. His pulse slowed. He thinks he is dying. But then, he rises from his hunched over position. He is not dead. Glancing into his reflection in a mirror, he sees his face is changing— right before his very eyes. His jaw line, eye color, and hair color. He watched in horror as his height and weight changed as well. He now possessed the ability to rapidly alter his cells on a molecular and nanoscale level to imitate anyone whom he had encountered in the history of his life. *A shapeshifter.*

Avalon became queasy as she recognized the face of the man in the images. It was her father. Dr. Adams. He boarded the habitat by pretending to be the President. She shuddered to contemplate what became of the real President. She willed herself to close off access to that part of his memory.

A huge smirk appeared on the President's face as he walked towards her.

Father? She cried with tears streaming down her face, still bowed down low to the ground in agony over her friends, many of whom were dying or dead.

Yes. I did all of this for you. So that we could inherit the Earth. Just us. Just the chosen few who deserve it.

This is wrong. All wrong! Can't you see that? Avalon shouted to him without moving her lips.

This is the only way. Don't you see? The only way to survive was to adapt to our new environment. Those that cannot adapt are doomed to extinction. This habitat provided both the time and the resources for me to finish the work I started. We are the new order.

Her father took her hand in his and kissed it with a big smile on his face. *I have always done, and will always do, anything to protect you.*

ACKNOWLEDGEMENTS

The Author would like to give thanks to God for the ability to write. I would also like to thank my parents for all of their emotional and financial support as I wrote this book. I could not have accomplished this without your help. Thank you to all of my extended family and friends who supported me on this endeavor, but specifically to my better half. This book would not have taken shape without your constant feedback and support. You are my alpha and beta reader and cheerleader wrapped in one. I would also like to thank my alpha reader, Anna, and my beta reader, Kate. Finally, heartfelt thanks to everyone who took a chance and purchased this book. I truly hope it brought you entertainment.

ABOUT THE AUTHOR

Nicole Stark studied English literature in college while drinking copious amounts of her favorite drink—coffee. She grew up reading a steady dose of Isaac Asimov, George Orwell, Madeline L'Engle, and Dr. Seuss. She blames these wonderful authors for transporting her to worlds far away from her day to day grind and helping inspire her to write. This is her debut novel.

Made in the USA
Monee, IL
26 April 2021